MADISON MORGAN
When Dogs Blog

PAM TORRES

This is a work of fiction. Names, characters, places, and incidents are either a product of the author's imagination or are used fictitiously. Any resemblance to actual persons, living or dead, events, or locales is entirely coincidental.

Author, Pam Torres is donating 10 percent of the proceeds from this book to the ASPCA®, animal shelters and other programs to benefit homeless or abused animals.

ISBN: 0615610951
ISBN 13: 9780615610955
LCCN: 2012934688
Legacy Media Press, Milton, WA

http://AnfinsenArt.blogspot.com

For information about ordering Madison in bulk for fundraising purposes please contact Project Madison at madison@madisonmorgan11.com

Acknowledgements

This book wouldn't have been possible if it weren't for the help and support of several people. This has become a family project and will leave a wonderful legacy for our entire family.

I'd like to dedicate this book to my only granddaughter Kayla and my four grandsons: Jaiden, Dylan, Lucas, Graysen and Dexter who I love very much. Kayla's love of animals, particularly dogs, manifested early in her life, inspiring Madison's story.

I want to thank Annie Crawford, an awesome writer, for her encouragement and editing skills. I thank my many beta readers Lillie, Lillian, Rae and Carol for helping me iron out the bumps.

I'm so excited that my mother, Carol Anfinsen was willing to create the wonderful painting for my lovely cover and sketches for the interior. They will be treasured by all of us.

I'm also very grateful for my supportive children who have told me repeatedly to pursue my dream of writing a book and had to sacrifice free babysitting so I could write. You're the bestest children and I love you.

Lastly, but definitely not the least of these is my dear friend, confidant, cheerleader, proof reader, adamant supporter and soulmate Andrew, who without his tender encouragement and belief in me, this project could never have come to fruition. Thank you, my love.

"The greatness of a nation and its moral progress can be judged by the way its animals are treated."

– Mahatma Ghandi

Chapter 1

"Madison, you'd better get moving!" Henry's voice echoed up the stairs. My eyes felt as if they were taped closed. The faint musky remnants of Mom's perfume hung in the air from the time I spilled it on the carpet. It happened when I was five; an innocent wish to wear her perfume ended in tears and a puddle on the floor. I thought Henry would have been angry, but he just cleaned it up in silence, tears streaming down his cheeks. That was when I knew he was more than my stepdad because he missed Mom as much as I did.

I willed my eyes open and blinked until I could focus. The pink curtains and wallpaper flowers looked stupid and babyish. My room has always been small, but today it was claustrophobic. My collection of stuffed dogs, all named and tagged, stared out from their shelves. They lost their appeal a while ago.

There isn't anything special about my house. I've lived in Bonney Lake my whole life—same street, same yard, same room—but something is different. Henry says change is inevitable and nothing lasts, but that's usually when he's missing

Mom. I can't explain it, but I just know I feel different. Henry thinks it's because I'm starting middle school, but that can't be. *#boring* [Hash tags are for Twitter, they can show a trend, but I use them whenever I want to emphasize a point. And not being excited about going back to school *is* the point.] Right? There is one thing I know: this is the year I'm going to get my very own dog.

I've wanted a dog forever. Seriously, I can't remember not wanting a dog. Henry doesn't think I'm ready. Whenever I bring it up, he switches on his instant-replay speech on responsibility. It's so predictable. By the time he's finished, my mind is numb. "Hello, anyone in there?" he asks, knocking his hand on whatever's close. He thinks it's funny—it's something from some old movie he loved. It just ticks me off. *#stupid*

Bad mood? Yep. I feel like this a lot. Henry says it's the beginning of my sardonic teen fog. Says it's normal. I disagree. I'm not even a teenager yet. I think there's something wrong with me, so I made a list of the reasons I don't feel normal (and by normal I mean I'm not like everybody else).

1. I don't have a mom. (Not a big deal, until now.)
2. I don't like boys; they're lame. Well, all the ones I know.

My best friend, Paige, used to speak the same language as me; sometimes we even knew what the other was going to say before the other one said it. Not anymore. Paige has a limited vocabulary: makeup, clothes, boys, the mall, and then more boys. Bottom line, she's lost her mind. I have no idea what she's talking about most of the time, nor do I care. *#boringx10*

Take last night, for example when Paige called I'd just figured out how to download a song from iTunes on Henry's computer.

"I can't decide...the green shirt...*mmm*...I wanna save that to wear with the skinny jeans...No wait, what about..."

"Sounds great. That'll work." My cursor moved in huge circles along with my eyes.

"What are you wearing?" she asked in that you-don't-get-it tone.

"I don't know yet—probably some clothes." I wanted to hang up. I hated talking into a piece of plastic, even if it was to my best friend.

"Very funny, Madison," she said, drawing out the words for emphasis. "This is the first day of middle school, and first impressions are huge. Ya don't want someone to think you don't care how you look."

Who took my best friend and left this fashionista officer in her place? "Hey, Paige, I really gotta go." It wasn't a total lie; I did have stuff to do.

"OK, meet you at the tree?" We've met at the huge sugar maple in Mr. Chervansky's yard since first grade. It was exactly forty-six and three-fourths steps from both our front doors. We know because we counted to make sure it was exactly halfway so it would be fair.

"Yep, see ya tomorrow." I pushed the end key and stuffed the phone in my pocket. I've only had my cell phone for a week. Henry finally gave in when I told him it would make it easier for him to keep track of where I am and who I'm with. He's always been interested, but now there's a different sound in his voice, like something bad is going to happen. Plus, now he wants to hang out with me all the time. Sometimes I just want to chill by myself. Then he gets this pouty lip and makes me feel all guilty, so I give in and watch something on TV with him.

OK, back to my list.

3. Everyone has a pet—everyone, that is, except me.
4. I'm supposed to be all excited about growing up and going to middle school, and I'm not.
5. I'm always grumpy. (Maybe I should work on that.)

The smell of coffee and toaster strudels wafted up the stairs. I'd have to finish my list later so I folded it over, creased it and slid it into my desk drawer. In the kitchen, Dad sat with the paper and his coffee mug.

"Good morning, sunshine! Milk or juice?"

"Juice, please."

"Comin' right up." I don't like talking in the morning. Henry, on the other hand, is just too wide-awake, too loud, and way too happy. "Are you ready for your first day of middle school? Are you excited?" He brought me a glass of juice and a plate of apple toaster strudels.

"Sure, I guess, a little."

"You should be. Not every sixth grader gets to pilot a laptop program. They've been talking about doing one for a number of years and you're just lucky that this is the year they decided to try it out. Do you think you'll get your computer today? I hear they're top of the line." Henry works at an architecture firm designing commercial buildings. The idea of another laptop in the house gets him all excited, mainly because I won't be bugging him to use his.

"I know, you told me." I took my last bite on the way to the sink; I was running late.

"Hold up, Madison. Aren't you forgetting something?" He had a pinched look to his face, the one that eventually leads to the pouty lip.

"Henry, seriously. I'm meeting Paige, and you know how she gets if I'm late. I still have to brush my teeth." I knew he just wanted a hug but I ran up the stairs instead. *#awkward*

I guess I should explain the whole Henry thing. Even though Henry is the only dad I've ever known, he isn't my real dad. I've always called him Henry, and at three, that was a hard name to learn. So when he and Mom got married it didn't make any sense to suddenly start calling him Dad. He says it's just a name, he knows he's my dad. Confusing? Maybe, but it works for us.

In the bathroom, I brushed my teeth and checked out the wonderful new red pimple on my chin. When I was little, my brown hair fell naturally into ringlets—cute on a three-year-old, not so much on an eleven-year-old. Not really an issue anymore, since the ringlets had become a thick mane of bushy waves. My options were:

1. Let it just be a wavy tangled mess.
2. Use the straight iron.
3. Use barrettes.

By the time I got the brush through it, I was too frustrated to spend any more time and whipped it into a ponytail. I said good-bye to Henry, making it as quick and painless as possible, and then I headed out to meet Paige.

We met the first day she moved into the neighborhood the summer after kindergarten. We spent every day that summer riding bikes and playing with her dachshund Barney, a long and wiry dog with deep brown eyes. I was so sad when he was hit by a car, you'd have thought he was my dog. I cried for a week.

"So, Madison, do you think there are any new boys this year?" Paige asked as we headed down Oak Avenue toward Hawthorne Junior High.

"I don't know." More alien talk. She's always saying stuff like, "Look at that one," or "I wonder how old he is." *#who-cares?*

"Well, it's time you started paying attention." She flipped her perfectly smooth blonde hair over her shoulder.

Loud barking broke the morning silence. Donald was hitting a fence with a stick to taunt a dog. He's always doing something annoying. I wanted to yell at him and tell him what an idiot he was, but I didn't because he's mean. The only thing worse than Donald teasing a dog is Donald teasing you, and I don't need that kind of attention—especially on the first day of middle school. *As a matter of fact, I'd be perfectly happy to go through this next year completely invisible. #strategicplan*

Chapter 2

When we arrived at Hawthorne, Paige and I went to room 111, our homeroom, and slid into the closest desks. There were a few new faces, a couple of girls at the back dressed a lot like Paige, and one boy I hadn't seen before. His tattered jacket with patched holes in each elbow, hung heavily on his shoulders and covered a dingy white T-shirt. His jeans, which piled on top of his shoes were obviously too large and held up by a thin black belt. Blond hair stuck out to one side of his head, like he'd just rolled out of bed. Bluish green eyes darted back and forth, and when they met mine, he looked away.

The teacher stood on her toes to reach the top part of the board, where she wrote her name, Ms. McBee. Wavy, light brown hair hung just above her shoulders. When she turned around, I was surprised at how young she was. She wore a light blue sweater over a collared shirt and dark blue pants. She slid on a pair of black-framed glasses and picked up the roll book.

"Good morning." No one was paying attention, and some students were still out of their seats. She waited until everyone settled down and found a desk.

"Good morning, class. Welcome to middle school. My name is Ms. McBee, but you can call me Ms. B. First, we need to take attendance." She rambled through the alphabet until she got to the M's.

"Paige Mahoney?"

"Here." Paige waved her hand like she was on a float in a parade.

"Cooper Mc—Nough—nan?" Ms. B stumbled.

"He-re." The new boy's voice cracked. Some muffled laughter hung in the air like a sour note.

Ms. B read off a few more names and then said, "Madison Morgan?"

"Here." I raised one finger.

After roll call, Ms. B checked out textbooks and—drum roll please—the laptops. They were black, shiny notebooks. Each one had a touchpad, but she said we could purchase a mouse if we preferred. I had to admit these laptops were pretty cool. They had cameras and tons of awesome software.

Our first assignment was to write a journal entry on… wait for it…summer vacation. *I know, big surprise.* Ms. B told us we'd eventually create a school blog where we could write posts and receive comments. She called it "building an online community."

By three thirty, my eyelids were heavy and my brain was fogged in. I must have nodded off because all of a sudden I heard a loud crash and realized I'd knocked a textbook off my desk. Donald leaned over. "Nice move, Grace."

I ignored him. *Way to go, Madison.*

I couldn't wait to get outside. Paige caught up to me. "What's the big hurry?" She shook her head. "Can't really meet anybody if you rush out like that."

"Who do you want to meet?" A reasonable question, I thought.

"Oh, Madison, you just don't get it. If we're going to get to know the older kids we have to hang, like they do."

"Hang and do what?" I asked.

"Talk."

I hate when she gives me that don't-you-know look. We walked to the front of the school, and Paige pretended she was waiting for someone. Then she smiled, laughed, and flipped her hair like I'd just said something funny.

I didn't know what was worse, pretending everyone was interested in us or heading home to the how-was-your-day interrogation. *I hate first days!*

Chapter 3

I paused before I opened the back door. I was 99.9 percent sure Henry would hit me with a bazillion questions about my first day, and my usual "fine" wouldn't be acceptable.

Most of the time, I'm glad he's home; but sometimes, like today, I wish he had a regular job and didn't get home until after five. I took a deep breath and plunged through the back door. Henry was at his computer talking to someone about permits or something. *Yes! I can dash upstairs and maybe skip the interrogation.*

"Not so fast, Bumblebee." Henry stood up and told the person on the phone that he'd call them back in two. He always says that, "back in two." Two what—days, hours, minutes? *And he gets mad when I'm vague.*

I braked and went back to the kitchen, plopped my backpack on the table, and slid into a chair. *If he calls me bumblebee again, I'm walking! #lame*

"So how was it?" he asked, settling in for his barrage of questions.

"How was what? I mean, what do you want to know?"

"Let's start with the computer. Is it in your backpack?" he said reaching for it.

"Yeah, it's pretty cool." This was a good place to start. Maybe I could get him interested in the new software and he'd forget about his probing. "You should see all the programs besides the word processor."

He carefully pulled the laptop from my backpack and opened it. I could tell he was impressed. He always gets this smirk like he knows something the rest of us don't.

"This is awesome. Do you have any projects yet?" he asked.

"Kind of. We have to write the proverbial what-I-did-this-summer paper. Tomorrow we're going to send the assignment to our class e-mail. From then on we will either e-mail or post our assignments to our online classroom website." I could tell he was listening. Could I slip in my regularly scheduled commercial for my own dog? Probably not. So far it hadn't gone anywhere.

"Ms. B talked all about responsibility and how not everyone in the school has this opportunity, and how it's because we're so responsible and all," I said, hoping he'd take the bait and admit I'm responsible.

"Yep, you're going to have to be extremely careful." He fiddled with the camera focus, his face growing and shrinking on the screen.

"So Dad, I was thinking, since I'm in middle school and older, don't you think it's about time I had my own dog?"

I always use Dad instead of Henry when I'm asking for something. As soon as it was out of my mouth it dropped to the floor like a popped balloon. I couldn't help but remember the summer goldfish incident. I was so worried that I'd forget to feed the fish that I decided I'd feed it every time I ate. One day I found the poor over-fed thing floating on its side, bloated and sick from too much food. *#badidea*

"You have a lot of new stuff going on—new school, new teachers, new computer—let's get used to these first." He closed the computer. I knew that the whole dog thing was closed too.

"Well, I need to get busy on that paper, so..." I grabbed my backpack and the computer right out of his hands and avoided his eyes.

"Dinner's in the oven. I'll let you know when it's time to set the table," he said as he picked up his phone. "Maybe we'll watch Animal Planet. I think there's a special about dogs tonight."

Oh, goody. I can have TV pets.

***

Animal Planet is one of the few TV stations that are in "Henry's system," along with the Discovery Channel and anything educational. MTV? Not so much. The program had already started; the background music sounded like a spy movie. The camera panned around an ordinary house that looked like it could use a new coat of paint, but it wasn't broken down and there were potted flowers on the porch. There were wire cages in the backyard, and as the camera got closer you could see the dogs, most of them on bare wire. There were way too many in a cage, and they didn't look healthy. The camera zoomed in on a small black and brown dog lying on her side, her fur matted and dirty. She looked into the camera, and her eyes were hazy and had goop around the edges.

"She was born a little over a year ago. She should be playing and romping, but she's too weak, too tired, too abused to move," the commentator said. "It's a shame, but for thousands of puppies this is their life, this is all they'll ever know."

I had a pain in my chest and I had to look away. It was the same pain I had when I saw Donald teasing that dog. Henry quickly switched off the TV.

"Thousands, really? Dad, that's a lot of puppies. Why do they do it?" It just didn't make any sense to me why anyone would do it.

"Money. They can make lots of money, pet stores can buy the dogs super cheap and then sell them for double, even triple the price."

"It's horrible. Is anyone doing anything about this?" I asked.

"There are some new laws that make it illegal in some states. So once the authorities uncover a puppy mill, people like Netta take the dogs and find new homes for them," he said. Netta runs a dog shelter out on Highway 17. I vaguely remember her from when I was little. We haven't been out there in years.

"How come we never see Netta?" We stopped going out there after Mom died, but Netta had come to the house one time. All I remember was she and Henry acted like strangers, which didn't make sense since Henry said Mom and Netta were friends—before. Everything changed when Mom died.

"Well, she's really busy and...we are, too. We'll get out there sometime, I'm sure."

Big surprise. Sometime, which really means never!

***

The next day Ms. B told us more about the blog. "If you're interested in helping to create a blog, I need to know and approve of your plan."

Paige looked at me. I knew she wanted to work together. The sad thing was I knew exactly what she'd want to blog about. *It isn't gonna happen.* No way was I going to do a blog on clothes and gossip. *I'd rather eat worms.* #superdumb

I wanted to blog about what I'd seen on Animal Planet, but I wasn't sure how to do it. I tried to write about it but it didn't seem as interesting as when I watched it. I'd have to learn more about what puppy mills were and why they existed.

The bell rang, so I closed my notebook before Paige could see what I wrote. She rushed over to my desk and tapped her foot while I finished packing my books. "You're always so pokey. The best time to meet people is in the hallway."

I looked up at her and realized she was serious. *Who appointed Deputy Paige to the sociability police?*

"Come on, Paige. Let's go get lunch before the line's too long." She trailed after me. Just before I entered the cafeteria, I heard a familiar voice.

"*Hmm*, smells like a dog, pants like a dog—must be a dog." Donald circled Cooper, the skinny new boy. Cooper turned to get away but Donald grabbed his brown jacket and whipped him around. Cooper lost his balance and fell. Everyone in the hallway laughed. I glared at Donald and then walked into the cafeteria. *What an über jerk!* Even though I had a twinge of guilt about walking away, at least my glare stopped Donald. *Remember the goal: invisibility.*

Chapter 4

Henry wasn't home. This would be a good time to plan my I-want-a-dog speech. I ran up the stairs to my room, pulled out a sheet of paper and wrote, *Why I Should Have a Dog,* and underlined it.

I'm ready for my own dog because I'm responsible.
I'm ready for my own dog so I can learn responsibility.

Wait a minute. How can I be responsible and need to learn responsibility? I erased the sentences, wiggled the pencil back and forth, and stared across the room as my mind wandered. The setting sun had turned the pink wallpaper flowers into orangey paintball splats that gave me a great idea: *Take the furniture out, cover the window, and shoot red and black paintballs all over the walls! #awesomeidea*

After staring at the paper until the lines blurred, I decided to number my dog ownership arguments and five seemed like the perfect number.

1. I'm ready to learn *more* responsibility, which means I'm old enough.
2. You and Mom had a dog. Why can't I?
3. I will walk the dog every day.
4. I will feed the dog every day.
5. I want a dog more than anything, and I won't be happy until I get one.

I wondered if the last one was too dramatic, but decided I'd leave it because I couldn't think of anything else and Henry's car had pulled into the garage. I took a deep breath and headed downstairs. When he came through the back door, I was at the kitchen table with the list in front of me. When I saw his face I decided I wouldn't read number five, even if it was true. He sat a large bag from Chan's Restaurant, our favorite Chinese take-out, on the counter and sat down.

"Hello. What's up, Madison?"

"Dad, I want to talk to you about getting a dog." I looked into his face for a reaction, but I didn't see one so I continued. "I've been thinking about it. I have five reasons why I think it's a good idea."

"OK, shoot," he said and sat down.

I read through my list. When I got to the fifth, I was surprised he hadn't stopped me but I rushed on, hoping to catch him off guard. "And Dad, I want a dog more than anything in this world, and I don't think I can go on without one."

Whoa, where did that come from? I felt a rock in the back of my throat and tears stung my eyes. I hoped my "theatrics" hadn't cost me. That's what Henry calls it when someone gets all upset over nothing. He just stared at the paper. I tapped my pencil and waited. *I'd definitely blown it.*

The goldfish incident popped into my head like a bad dream. The morning I discovered Stanley floating at the top of the bowl, his eyes bugged out, I screamed and Henry burst into my room. He grabbed me when he found me curled around the fishbowl, sobbing and choking; he thought I was suffocating, or worse, having a heart attack. He screamed my name. I couldn't speak so I pointed to Stanley. His eyes rested on the dead fish, and then he looked back at me and hurried out of the room. Only much later did he help me flush Stanley down the toilet. I insisted on music and made him read a poem I'd written.

> Stanley, you were a good friend.
> Stanley, we will miss you.
> Stanley died, and Mom did too.

It was the stupidest poem, but I was only five. Still, Henry cried. After that we didn't go to the pet store or the zoo for a long time. When I asked for a new fish, Henry said I wasn't ready. I knew it wasn't me. He was the one who wasn't ready.

"Madison," he said quietly. "I can see you've thought about this for a while. I need to think about it, too."

I couldn't tell if this was good or bad. Parents always say they'll think about it when they don't want to discuss something. *Why is it OK for parents to be vague? #totallyunfair*

"How long? Ten minutes? An hour?" I thought it was a fair question because I was sure it was just a stall.

"I don't know, but when I'm ready I'll tell you. Now would you set the table, please?" He gathered his things and went up to his room.

That's it? Are you kidding me?

"Sure, Dad." It would be stupid to push. There are two things I know about Henry: One, when he doesn't want to talk about something, he tunes out. And two, those things almost always have to do with Mom. I'm not sure what having a dog has to do with my mom, except that they had a dog, but it might explain why he's avoiding it. I get that it makes him sad to remember her; it makes me sad, too. *But he doesn't understand I need to know her. I need to feel her near me.*

Chapter 5

Only a few days had gone by since I'd given Dad my list, and I couldn't think of anything else. I thought of it at home, while I did my homework, and even when I was at school, which had cost me. I was quickly collecting points toward some detention. Henry hadn't said a thing, and I began to wonder if he would. Once I asked him if I could cut my hair, and it took him two whole weeks to give me an answer, and by then I'd changed my mind. Nothing would change my mind this time. *I wanted…no, I needed a dog.*

In class, Ms. B droned on about Jim Carr and Commencement Bay and other Washington State history. We'd been assigned to take notes on our laptops. I just kept typing *My Own Dog* with exclamation points all the way down my screen and hoped the teacher wouldn't ask me to read my notes.

"*Psst*, Madison." Paige leaned in while Ms. B wrote on the board. "Did you see Pete this morning?" Pete was Paige's new I-just-think-he's-so-cute flavor-of-the-week.

"No, Paige." I shook my head and rolled my eyes, just in time for Ms. B to catch it.

"You disagree, Madison?" she asked. *You're so gonna pay for this, Paige!*

"*Uuhhh*, no, it's not about that."

"Perhaps you'd like to share it with the rest of the class?"

"No, ma'am. Sorry." I slumped farther into my chair. *So much for being invisible.*

After class, Paige grabbed my arm and yanked me into the hall to show me Pete. "See?" she said. "Doesn't he look cute with his new haircut?"

I pulled my arm away. Was she out of her mind? Friendship guilt quickly replaced my irritation. "I'm sorry, Paige. You startled me."

***

When I got home, I was eager to tell Henry my idea for the blog. "Dad, I've figured out what I want to write in the blog I told you about, and—" I stopped when I saw the look on his face. You know the one—where one eyebrow lifts higher than the other. It meant I was in for a lecture.

"That's all well and fine, but you still have to take care of your regular responsibilities." He pulled the dishwasher door open. I'd forgotten I was supposed to empty it that morning.

"Sorry Dad, but I was in a real hurry, and I forgot. What's the big deal, anyway? I'm here now; I can do it." I knew he wasn't going to like what I'd said, but geez, why can't he let me mess up? *Why do I always have to be perfect? #Henry'sSystem*

I should explain something about Henry. He's all about organization and schedules. Sometimes I want to call him Captain Henry. I'd never do it, though; that would hurt his feelings. It's just that most of the time I feel more like an employee than a daughter.

"Madison, we have a system. If the system fails, then we have chaos." Chaos actually sounded good. I knew Henry was trying not to yell at me because he has a habit of clenching his jaw. Once when he was talking to an obviously annoying client. I was behind him and couldn't help but notice his butt muscles tense and I was pretty sure it was tight now.

"You'd think I was taking drugs or stealing money. It's the dishes; I'll do it now. Geez." Sometimes I want to take his system and shatter it into a million pieces. He thinks everything is like those buildings he designs, with systems running smoothly the same way at the same time every day. I think he forgets I'm not one of his buildings but a person with my own ideas, and I'm getting older.

"All right, Madison, settle down. Let's not overreact." He came over to help with the dishwasher. *Seriously, who's overreacting?*

"So what did you want to tell me?" he asked. It didn't seem all that important anymore. The stubborn part of me wanted to keep it to myself, but I knew it would feel like an epic daughter fail if I did.

"I've been working on a blog post that Ms. B said I could write for the school blog."

"That sounds great. Do you know what you want to write?"

"I'm thinking about that show we saw on Animal Planet. You know, the puppy mills, but I just don't know enough about it. You said that people like Netta get involved. She probably knows all about it." I paused to see what he'd say. Even giving me a phone number would be better than nothing.

"Maybe we could take a trip out to her rescue shelter sometime." There was that word again—*sometime*—the one that usually means not anytime soon.

"That would be nice," I said, placing the last bowl on the shelf. What else could I say? It wasn't like he was planning an actual trip out there. This was just another Henry stall.

Chapter 6

The next morning I woke up sweating, and knew I'd had the dream again. I started having it a year ago. Sometimes it's at night, and all I see is moonlight shimmering off dark water. Other times the sun is so bright that I squint as the reflection dances off the waves. There's always a dog with midnight black hair peeking over the edge of a red washtub. In each dream I reach my hands out and stretch my fingertips but I barely touch the red tub as it washes past. Then I wake up all sweaty and breathing hard. I'm totally weirded out by it. It doesn't make any sense. First of all, why would a dog get in a washtub in the first place? And second, I don't know any dog that would stay in one.

Dad's singing voice echoed up the stairs, and when I got to the kitchen he was busy setting the table. It's way too early for "Seventy-six Trombones," some song from an old musical. If you don't know what that is, count yourself lucky. Henry loves brass instruments like trumpets and stuff, so this is one of the songs he regularly drives me crazy with.

"Morning, Dad. Think you could turn it down a little? I'm not even awake yet." I slid into my chair and placed my head on the table.

"Come on, Madison, it's a great day. The sun's out."

Why was he in such a good mood? My morning hadn't gone so great. I couldn't get a knot out of the underside of my hair; it's on my neck behind my ear. *Why couldn't Mom have left me her smooth, straight locks along with her blue eyes?*

"Here's your lunch, Maddy—whoops, Madison." Henry said as he sat a brown paper bag on the table next to me. I quietly spooned a bite of Cheerios into my mouth.

I've decided I want to go by Madison now that I'm in middle school. Maddy sounds kind of girly, and I'm just not a girly-girl. Fighting with my hair this morning took long enough—there was no way I was staying in front of the mirror to put on makeup. Paige tried to get me to wear some, but it just made me itchy and she'd poked me in the eye. *Why do girls wear that sticky stuff?* #girlfail

***

During last period I received a note that Dad was in the office to pick me up. He hadn't done this since Mom passed away and he came from the hospital, so my throat was dry and I couldn't swallow as I walked to the office.

Dad was signing me out when I got there. "What's up, Dad?"

"I want to show you something," he said. He put his arm around me and we walked out to the car. There in the backseat sat a tiny dog. Its pink tongue hung from a panting jaw, and dark eyes looked up at me.

"What's that?"

"Madison, this is Lilly. She needs a home, and I thought you'd like to take care of her for a while." He looked at me, and I knew he was waiting for me to scream, jump up and down—something.

"What do you mean, for a while?" I looked at the dog. Wispy black and brown hair covered its scrawny body. Not exactly the kind of dog I had envisioned.

"Lilly is a rescue and needs a temporary home. It's just until Netta can find a permanent one for her." He opened the door and motioned for me to climb in next to her.

I hesitated; this wasn't how I wanted to get a dog. I would only be babysitting this one. I slid into the back seat, shut the door and squished myself as far away from the dog as possible.

All the way home, I kept looking at her and then at my dad. I just couldn't figure it out. *What the heck was Henry thinking?* For one thing, I wasn't prepared; for another, we hadn't even talked about it; and for a third thing—and this was the biggie—I didn't even choose this dog. Every time Lilly tried to get closer, I pushed her away and she'd whimper. The sadder she looked, the worse I felt.

As soon as we entered the kitchen, Dad said, "We need to discuss what Lilly needs and how we can help her get ready for a new home."

"Right." I looked at the floor. I was sure if I looked at Dad I'd either start bawling or yelling, and since I didn't know which, I avoided his eyes altogether.

"Madison, what's wrong?"

Tears flooded my eyes in spite of my effort. "Seriously? You didn't even talk to me about this. I wasn't even involved. This is your dog, not mine." *He just doesn't get it.*

"I'm sorry you feel that way. We can talk about this later. Right now I'm going to take Lilly for a walk, which she desperately needs after being in the car so long." Dad hooked the leash to Lilly's collar and went out the door.

I sat at the table and thought about what had happened. I was so frustrated with myself for my uncontrolled emotion, but I was also mad. Dad had done what he always does: he fixed what he thought was the problem. He never even talked to me. What am I, a building that needs an adjustment here or there? Doesn't he understand that I'm responsible and ready for my own dog? Instead, he hands me a lollipop and tells me to be quiet.

Chapter 7

When I woke the next morning, I felt a warm bundle on my feet. Startled, I kicked and then realized it was Lilly. She yelped, peed on my floor, and ran. *Oh, great! This is going to be an awesome day.*

It was Saturday, and knowing Henry, he'd planned the entire day. He loves Saturdays. He says they're catchup day; whatever didn't get done during the week can be done then. I think that's where I get my list habit. There's always a list.

When I got downstairs, Dad was already gone. The note at the top of the list said:

We'll talk when I get back.

- Feed and water Lilly.

- Take Lilly for a walk.

- Clean out dishwasher.

- Sweep floor.

- Grocery shop: I've got this one, Madison.

Usually the Saturday list was longer, but maybe he'd add to it later. Lilly sat on the floor beside her empty bowl. There was a bag of dog food on the counter, so I poured a little into her dish. Lilly gulped it down. Then I filled her water bowl. Lilly growled in fear, and it surprised me that I knew exactly what she was trying to say. I took my hand back and sat calmly on the floor. For a moment I had a strange feeling in the pit of my stomach. It reminded me of the time I'd wandered away from Dad at the store and one of the sales clerks came toward me. Fear. The little dog was frightened, and I felt bad that she was afraid of me. *I might not want her, but it isn't her fault.*

My phone bleeped. There was a text from Dad asking if I wanted anything from the store. I texted: "Nope." He's just trying to be nice, hoping I'll forgive him. I won't.

I finished my cereal and snapped the leash onto Lilly. We headed down the street. She stopped to smell something every couple of minutes. The tightness in my stomach had relaxed, and I knew Lilly's had, too.

We rounded the corner of the next block, and I noticed someone walking in our direction. When we got closer, I saw that it was the new boy, Cooper. I hadn't seen him since the day Donald pushed him in the hallway.

He wore the same white T-shirt—or at least one like it—and a pair of baggy jeans. His pace was slow, as if he didn't have anywhere to go. When we were close enough Lilly nosed around his shoes and then stopped and backed away, her tail tucked between her legs and her head lowered. My stomach tightened like a twisted rubber band.

"Hi, Cooper," I said. Lilly peeked out from behind my feet.

"Hi, Madison." He crouched down to let Lilly smell him, but it didn't make a difference. She still hid.

"I'm sorry. She's afraid." I don't know how I knew, but I knew.

"Oh, it's OK. Sometimes I do that to dogs," he said and shrugged his shoulders. He tried again to coax her out and patted her head. He stood up, his head bent, and he shoved his hands in his pockets. His clothes were wrinkled, like they'd just been picked up off his floor. Cooper looked at me like he was going to say something but stopped before it could escape his lips. His eyes didn't look sad, just empty… and lonely.

"Well, gotta go." He turned to go down a long gravel driveway.

"All right, then. See ya on Monday." Lilly and I continued to the end of Stuart Street and then turned around to head back home. When we got back to where Cooper had turned off, Lilly hesitated. My palms began to sweat, and my heart beat so hard I could feel it in my throat. I peered down the gravel driveway that swung around the side of Cooper's green house. I felt pulled, like there was something coaxing me forward. I took a step, the gravel crunched under my shoe, but Lilly planted her paws. I knew I'd have to drag or carry her, so I gave up. I thought

I could hear dogs barking from behind the house. I decided Lilly was just a scaredy-cat when it came to other dogs, but that didn't explain my shaky knees.

My phone buzzed. It was Dad. His text said, "I'm home. Lunch is ready. Love you."

When we walked in the door, I made sure Lilly had water and then knelt down and looked into her eyes. They seemed to be asking me a question, I was sure of it, but I didn't know what it was. *Maybe she isn't as dumb as I thought.*

***

Things changed over the next few days, and Dad noticed. "Looks like you and Lilly have made a connection."

"Something like that. Let's just say we have an understanding." I didn't want to let him know that my feelings toward her had changed. I was still angry with him for not including me in the decision in the first place, but I'd accepted the fact that it wasn't Lilly's problem. It was mine.

Mine and Henry's.

In my room that night I thought about whether I wanted to participate in the class blog that Ms. B had suggested. The idea was cool, but it meant that everyone would be reading what I wrote. That made me uncomfortable. Besides, I was already having a hard time with Paige; this could just make it worse. The other day she'd texted that she wanted to work together on a blog idea: we could take pictures of ourselves in different outfits and write about them. *Seriously? Not going to happen. #lame*

Lilly was across the room licking her paws one by one. She stopped when she realized I was staring at her. That's it—I could write about Lilly. It could be a journal about my foster dog and what we did.

The next day, since I'd brought a cold lunch, I met with Ms. B during lunch to talk about the blog. "I'm kind of nervous about having my writing out there for everyone to see," I said.

"I understand," Ms. B said. "It can be scary to put your thoughts out there for strangers to read, but it gets easier. The important thing right now is to decide what you want to say."

"Well, I thought writing about my new foster dog would be a good idea."

She smiled and sat on the desk beside me. "I think you've come up with a great idea. You could start by describing how you feel about having a foster dog."

"At first I thought it was stupid. Why would I want a dog that wasn't really mine? I still want my own dog, but I found out about all the dogs that need homes and how hard it is for them to find them, especially if they've only lived in a kennel. I read on a website that it's important they get used to people and other dogs."

"It sounds like this is something you're passionate about." She looked at me with brown eyes as warm as honey.

"I could write about what happened every day. Lilly is always doing something funny or weird. At the same time, I could talk about fostering. Maybe somebody else would be interested in doing it. Maybe I could help." I felt my brain spin with ideas. *This might be fun! #actuallyexcited*

"Madison, why don't you go ahead and write your first blog post, and tomorrow after school you and I can post it. What do you think?"

"I can do that." I pulled out my pen and wrote "Blog Post" at the top of my paper.

"Hold on; it's time for math, but I'm sure you'll have some free moments before tomorrow." She stood up just as the rest of the class returned from lunch.

I heard Donald taunting Cooper about sleeping with the dogs. *What's he talking about? Why doesn't he just leave him alone?*

Donald is like a hovering buzzard, always looking for someone else to bother. He's relentless in his taunting of Cooper. Yesterday, Cooper finally said he didn't have a dog and turned his back, but Donald just kept following him down the hall.

I gave him my dirtiest look, but he just laughed. Cooper looked confused but seemed relieved when Donald went back to his desk. One of these days I knew I wouldn't be able to stay quiet. Something inside of me starts to bubble when someone is unfair. *I think that someday it might boil over.*

Chapter 8

There was a lot to do before I'd be ready to post the blog. First, I had to see if I could set up a time to talk to Netta. That could be a challenge, since Henry acts like her house is so far away and it's a hassle to take the drive out there. Somehow, I have to talk him into it. Now that it's a school project, he might be more willing.

I was concerned because our last full conversation hadn't been pleasant. Making the decision about Lilly without me was just plain wrong. *Why couldn't I go out to the kennels myself?* I was still pretty mad at him, but I had to get past that to make him understand that talking to Netta was important for my project.

When I walked through the door, Lilly wasn't waiting for me by the door and her leash was gone. That meant Dad was home and had taken Lilly for her walk. I decided I'd better do something, so I rinsed the dishes in the sink and stacked them in the dishwasher, and then headed upstairs to work on the blog.

The more I thought about the blog, the more excited I was to start it. I looked at the form Ms. B had e-mailed me and started filling it out.

Blog Project: Foster dog diary.

Blog Purpose: My experiences with Lilly, my foster dog—the good and the bad.

Then I typed in my first blog entry.

First Day: The day I met Lilly, I didn't know that I was going to be taking care of a dog, let alone one that I couldn't keep. Man, was I ~~pissed~~ mad. When I thought about getting a dog, I thought about going to buy a puppy. You know, in a pet store. I wanted to pick it out. When my dad just brought her home, I didn't like her at first. She wasn't a puppy, and she wasn't the kind of dog I'd been dreaming of. She was scrawny, wouldn't sit and was afraid of her own shadow. When I got close, she would shy away like I was going to hit her. What was up with that? I tried really hard not to like her, but truthfully it was difficult. What can you do when a fuzzy little muzzle rubs up against your leg and big brown eyes stare into yours? Nothing, it's all over.

I thought this was a good start, and I hoped that Henry would agree. Then I'd tell him about my ideas for other posts: an interview with Netta at her kennel, and training and caring for Lilly. I had to wait for the right time, but I was ready.

***

"You're right, you know," Dad said out of the blue. We had been watching television in silence. We hadn't made any effort to talk, and I thought neither of us would back down—we're stubborn that way—so I was surprised he said anything.

"What?" I asked.

He turned to me and said it again. "You're right. I shouldn't have brought Lilly home without first talking to you about it. To be honest, I don't know why I didn't."

"I know. You don't think I'm responsible; and worse, you're still treating me like a little girl," I blurted. That was stupid, but I couldn't help how I felt. Lilly, who'd been curled up on her pillow, stood up and came over to my feet, turned a few circles, and plopped down. I felt a tug on the inside of my chest and knew she was anxious and worried.

"Some of that might be true." He stood up and walked across the room to the built-in bookcases. We used to sit on the floor and pull one book after another from the shelves. He told me more than once that even if there was a leaky basement and holes in the roof, Mom had to have this house. She loved the bookcases.

He reached up and moved a large red clay bowl off to one side and pulled out small tin box. I'd never noticed it way up on the top shelf. The paint had chipped off in most places, and it had a big clasp on the front.

"This was your mother's," he said, sitting down next to me. For a moment we both just stared at the box. It had been a long time since we'd spoken about Mom.

"What is it?" I asked as I rubbed my finger across the top. There were flower patterns pressed into the tin.

"Inside are clippings, small trinkets, and other things that your mom collected. She started when she was about your age. She wanted you to have it." He handed it to me, and I felt the reverence that he had for it, like it was a part of her that he couldn't touch.

I took the box; the thin tin felt cool in my hands. "Thanks, Dad. Should I open it?" Lilly stood and placed her paws on my knees.

"That's your call, Madison." He lightly rested his hand on my shoulder. "It was important to your mother that you have it. She told me I would know when it was time."

"How do you know?" I looked up at his face. His eyes were watery. He cleared his throat when he realized I was looking at him.

"I just know," he said.

Chapter 9

During school on Wednesday, I was minding my own business and doodling when Donald came and hovered over my desk like a hawk over its prey. "So, what's up with you and Cooper?" he asked, tapping his finger on my shoulder.

"What are you talking about?"

"I haven't seen him, and I depend on him for lunch money." He bent over and put his face in front of mine, his hands on my desk. Had he seen Cooper stop me in the hall after class? He'd only stuttered my name and hadn't managed to get anything out. My stomach felt queasy, and I hoped that he wouldn't notice my tapping foot—a sure sign I'm nervous.

"Why would I know anything about Cooper? It's not like we hang out or anything. I've only talked to him twice." I hoped he would move on to torture someone else.

"We have unfinished business, and I don't want him wimping out." He chuckled and sauntered over to his desk and pushed himself into the chair, a smug grin plastered across his face. I hate that grin; it made me anxious, because behind it were the eyes of someone just waiting to pounce.

It was true, though. Cooper hadn't been at his desk for a few days now. I tried to remember the last time I'd seen him. It had been last Monday afternoon when I was out walking Lilly.

Ms. B waved me over to her desk. "Madison, I hope you won't mind, but I thought it'd be nice if Cooper worked on the blog with you."

"I guess so," I said. *Of course, he would actually have to show up at school.*

"This is the deal, Madison. I've noticed that he hangs around after school is over, sometimes until it's almost dark." She glanced over at Cooper's empty chair. "At least this would give him something to do."

Now I'm a babysitter?

On the way home, Paige went on and on about how she'd talked to Katie in her PE class. "So then she said she thinks he's so cool. And then I said yeah, and then she asked me what my favorite song was. It was so awesome—like we were real friends and everything." Paige was almost on her toes as she gave me the play by play. *Unbelievable. How did I survive without this important piece of information?*

"That's nice." I swear if she tells me they exchanged lipsticks or fashion secrets, I might be sick.

"She said that maybe tomorrow we could sit by her group at lunch. Isn't that so nice?" She was genuinely excited that they might grant us the privilege of dining near them. *#lame*

"You know, Paige, I just don't see what the big deal is—"

"This is huge! Sitting at a lunch table with seventh graders—it's like, well, like we're in, you know?" I could tell she was serious. I pinched my lips tight to keep them from bursting into an obnoxious laugh.

"Wow, Paige. I'm so glad we've been approved." I tried to sound sincere but it just wasn't possible. She saw through it.

"Oh, never mind. You just don't get it. Whatever." She rolled her eyes at me. We didn't talk the rest of the way home, and she didn't even turn to say good-bye when I split off to go down my driveway.

"Bye, Paige. See ya tomorrow." I watched her walk down the street and wondered if things would ever be the same.

Chapter 10

I GRABBED THE LEASH OFF THE HOOK AND CALLED LILLY. WHEN SHE came I stared into her shiny, round eyes. Her open acceptance poured over me like a warm shower. Something in me had changed, and I knew that we were friends. Even though I'd been cold and indifferent, Lilly wasn't going to hold that against me. I had a friend who liked me just the way I was.

I took my usual route down Maple, past Paige's. I had just rounded the corner of Elm and Stuart when I heard footsteps behind me. It was Cooper.

"Do you always sneak up on people?" I said, and Lilly darted around my legs and poked her head between them.

"Well, *uhh*...no. I didn't know what to say." Cooper fidgeted with his shirtsleeve.

"How about, 'hey Madison,'" I said, giving him that are-you-kidding-me look. I could tell he was self-conscience by the way he rocked from side to side. It made me nervous. Lilly was still crouched behind my legs. "Look, I don't know where you've been, but there are people worried about you."

"I'm sorry." He stared at the ground with an occasional glance to my face. He bit his lip, and I could tell he did it often because it was red and chapped.

"So, the other day, you know, when I met you at the end of your driveway, I kind of followed you." This made him even more nervous, and he started picking at an invisible thread on his sleeve. "Look, it's OK, I didn't go far. I was just going to the end of the street, but I couldn't help looking down your long driveway. I thought I heard dogs barking. Lilly wouldn't budge so I couldn't get any closer. Do you have dogs?"

"Yeah, we have some. Why?" His face turned white like his T-shirt.

"Oh, nothing really. It's just the other day when Donald teased you about having a dog but you said you didn't have one." I guess it really wasn't any of my business, but why would somebody lie about having dogs?

"I…don't have…a…dog. My uncle has dogs."

"Oh, OK. What kind of dogs does your uncle have?" Lilly walked around and sat next to my legs instead of between them.

"Why?" He squinted like he didn't trust me. I was beginning to feel like I was talking to a shy four-year-old, coaxing the words out of him.

"OK, OK, I get it. I just thought it was something we might have in common. Sorry I asked." *#whatever*

"I'm sorry, I just..." He pulled on his sleeve again.

"It's fine. Oh, by the way, Ms. B wants you to work on the class blog with me after school on Wednesdays. Of course, you'll have to show up to school. I already wrote the first one, but you can help with the next one."

"What's it about?"

Could he actually be interested? "Foster dogs. It started as a day-in-the-life thing about Lilly and me. I really want to interview this lady at the shelter where my dad got her." His eyes opened wider, and Lilly nosed around the grass at his feet.

"I think I know her. Does she run the Second Chance dog shelter out on Highway 17? I think her name is Nanette or something," he said.

"That's the one. Do you actually know her?" By now, Lilly had relaxed and sat panting on the grass between us.

"Yeah, I bring her...strays." He stopped short.

"You've been out there?"

"It's only an hour bus ride." He shrugged like it was no big deal. *Maybe working with Cooper wouldn't be totally lame.*

"Would you be willing to go with me sometime?" I blurted without thinking.

"I guess so." He tugged his shirt down over his jeans.

"We'd have to go during school. My dad would never let me go." It seemed impossible. *A plan...we need a plan.*

"If we took the eight o'clock bus to Seattle..." Cooper paused and looked up as he bit his bottom lip. "We could take the the two o'clock bus back. It would drop us right in front of the school right when it gets out."

Could this actually work? It all sounded good, and the excitement rose inside me like a pot beginning to simmer. "When...when could we go?" *Breathe Madison, breathe.*

"I can go anytime; it's up to you." Cooper looked at me intently. His deep blue eyes seemed to pierce through me, and I had to look away.

"Well, today's Wednesday...what about Friday? My dad usually has meetings in the city, so he won't be home until late afternoon." I made a mental note to erase any messages left by the school. I'd never skipped school before, so the thought made me feel all bubbly inside. "We'll have to cut down Stuart and then over to Bingham. I'm afraid if Paige saw me she'd rat us out, especially since she's been sort of mad at me lately." I hoped Cooper couldn't see that I was trembling just at the thought of breaking a rule. Besides, I wasn't sure if I was ready for anyone to see us together. It was one thing to have a project after school but quite another to be spending time outside of school.

"We could take the back way on the trail behind the school. No one would see us then," Cooper suggested. I'd only been on that trail once with Dad. He made me promise I would never go on it without him, because the dark trees make it invisible from any homes or roads.

"Then it's settled. I'll meet you at the end of Maple." Now that it was a real plan and I had committed myself to it, the simmering slowed and my hands stopped sweating. I decided it was the right thing to do, even though I knew it'd mean lying to Henry. That part gave me a queasy yuck in the pit of my stomach, but not enough to dampen my excitement. The question now was could I actually go through with it?

Chapter 11

On Friday morning, I jumped and hit the lamp when Dad knocked on my door to make sure I was awake.

"You OK in there?" he asked.

"Yeah. Down in a minute." He'd scared the crap out of me. At least I'd slept; at two o'clock I'd wondered if I'd ever sleep.

I knew that if I could just get through this morning then the rest would be easy. All I had to do was act normal. *Do I ever act normal?*

When I got downstairs, Henry was already packing up to go.

"Madison, remember I might be later than usual tonight. I have that meeting in the city." He picked up his laptop and headed for the door. I followed him and gave him a hug. Lilly rubbed up against both our legs almost like she knew I felt guilty and hoped I'd change my mind. *#noway*

***

The air was crisp and the sky was clear, so I took a deep breath and told myself that this was a good sign. By the time I got to the end of Maple, Cooper was already there. We headed down Stuart without saying a word. I was replaying the morning to make sure I hadn't done anything to tip Dad off that I wasn't going to school today.

"Sorry, Cooper. I haven't skipped school before, and I'm a little bit jumpy."

"It's fine. I don't talk much in the morning anyway." Cooper's breath floated from his mouth into the cold air.

"Me either. My dad always wants to chat, and I like waking up quietly." We continued down the road silently. When we got to the trailhead, I stopped and let Cooper go first. I thought I'd feel scared going down the trail without my dad, but with Cooper I didn't feel afraid at all. We'd barely stepped off the trail when Cooper broke into a run in the opposite direction of the school.

"Come on! We must be late or the bus is early!" He pointed to the bus approaching at the end of the street, the opposite direction of the school. We ran and barely made it up the steps to pay our fares. We tumbled into our seats and sighed, relieved we hadn't missed our ride. Even better, no one had seen us.

We'd been on the bus for ten minutes when Cooper looked at me and spoke. "There's a reason your dog Lilly… doesn't like me." He paused and looked at his hands.

"OK, I'm listening." I didn't mean to, but I sounded mad. *#grumpypants*

"She knows me." He fiddled with the zipper on his brown jacket— the one he wore every day, even when it wasn't cold.

"What do you mean, she knows you?" His frequent pausing made me impatient. I took a deep breath and tried to relax.

"It's, well...I know how Netta found her. I know what happened to her...I know because I'm the one that made sure she got to Netta." Cooper's voice was shaky and his eyes were glazed. This time I waited for him to finish. "She—Lilly...her real name is...I mean *was* Dizzy. I called her that 'cause when she was a puppy she ran around and around in her cage."

"I'm confused. What are you talking about?" This didn't make any sense, and I was frustrated. I'm not good with riddles, and this was starting to sound like one.

"I just felt sorry for her. I just didn't want her to end up like..." He took a deep breath and blurted, "Because if I didn't she'd be dead, she'd have been stuck there and I couldn't let that happen." By then he was choking back sobs. I was embarrassed and wasn't sure what to do next.

"OK, wait. Take a breath." I sounded just like Henry. "First, what do you mean, she'd be dead?"

Cooper looked at the floor and kicked the back of the seat in front of us. I hadn't ever noticed how dirty his shoes were or the ragged ends of his laces. When he didn't answer, I filled the silence with another question.

"I don't understand. What would have happened to her if you hadn't taken her to Netta?"

"I wanted Dizzy—I mean Lilly—to have it better. You know, get a better home." He looked at me. "That's why I put her on Netta's porch. I don't really know Netta, or actually she doesn't know me."

"I don't understand." His story had as many holes as a piece of Swiss cheese. "How did you know her name was Nanette?"

"When I called, she answered the phone and said it."

"So where—?"

"It isn't a good place," he said as he turned in his seat and stared out the window. The leaves were barely showing color and would deepen as the air got colder. He must have decided that the conversation was over.

I don't know why I did it, but I put my hand on his knee and patted a few times. He looked at me with a half smile and I knew that he'd tell me more when he was ready.

"I won't say anything, if that's what you're worried about." With nothing left to say, we rode in silence until Cooper said that the next stop was Netta's.

Chapter 12

Cooper pointed at the large gate as we stepped from the bus, and we both stopped. I needed to relax, but the shivers spread to my jaw as soon as the cold air hit my lungs.

"This is it," Cooper said, as we headed for the gate. When we were standing in front of the gate Cooper took in a deep breath and said, "Here goes." We opened the gate and headed down the gravel driveway. Large trees cast shadows across the gravel and blocked the view of Netta's house from the street—a good thing since it was painted Pepto-Bismol pink. The in-the-kennel sign hung on the door. "Kennel" was crossed out and "red barn" was written in black marker, so we went around to the back and found three buildings. The red barn was small compared to the other buildings and much older. It took both of us to push the heavy barn door open. Our noses filled with the smell of warm, wet dog hair; straw; and old wood.

"Hey, shut the door, guys. I have a litter of puppies back here, and it's cold out there." Netta's voice was shrill, but it didn't hurt our ears. I wondered what she'd sound like when she was mad. Cooper looked at me with his oh-no-what-are-we-doing-here blue eyes. *Wasn't this his idea?*

"Netta, it's me, Madison. Where are you?" There was a damp musty smell, straw was scattered on the floor. Wood posts marked off aisles. I headed down the first one. Cooper didn't say anything and kept his eyes glued to the ground in front of him.

"Madison? Back here, dear. Just follow the second aisle down to the end," she yelled. A few puppies yelped when they heard her voice. We headed down the second aisle and found Netta on the ground with a litter of young puppies, all black except for one with white paws. She rolled the small puppies over on her hand and then put them back with their mother.

"What are you doing?" I asked.

"Oh, these little fellas were born yesterday, and I'm just checking them over and making sure they're all healthy. It's important to handle puppies in the first few days—helps them be calm and relaxed with humans. Just routine." Netta jumped up and wiped her hands on the rag thrown over the stall gate. Then she whipped her arms around me and squeezed me super tight. Her black hair stuck out from under the faded pink bandana around her head. She wore a bright, lime green shirt that said "Groovy Girl" across the front. "You've grown so big! So what brings you both all the way out here?"

"Netta, this is Cooper. Cooper, Netta." Cooper nodded in her direction, and she stepped forward and shook his hand. Cooper stood there, his body as stiff as his hand.

"We're working on a—"

"Let's head over to the house; it'll be more comfortable there," she interrupted and headed for the door.

We followed her out to the house and into the kitchen. Big, tall cabinets lined the walls, and the dark wood table was piled with mail that Netta started scooping up and dropping onto a chair. Most of the counters were stacked with boxes and bags of dog food. Dirty dishes filled the sink, and the stove was coated with spills and grime. She pulled up a chair at the table, and Cooper and I did, too. I knew he was really scared, so I did all the talking.

"We're working on a class project—a blog. And...well, we wanted to ask you about what you do here and where you get the dogs, like Lilly." I noticed that Cooper was fidgeting with his zipper again.

"Oh, good grief, where are my manners? Can I get you something to drink? There's water, chamomile tea, and a new dandelion punch I made just yesterday." *#yuck* Cooper and I both shook our heads. "Lilly was one of those dogs that get left on my doorstep. It doesn't happen often, but when it does I'm usually full to capacity in the kennels. I really appreciate your dad taking her." She poured a glass of green-tinted liquid for herself and then looked at me. "Does your dad know you're here?"

"Oh, sure, of course." I hadn't realized that every time you tell a lie it gets easier to repeat it. "I guess it'd be good to know all the other places your dogs come from." I opened my notebook and pulled the pen out of my back pocket. Cooper sat and stared at the floor. *This is the part where I do all the work. #bigsurprise*

"It depends. I think the most common reason I get dogs is because people don't really know why they wanted a dog in the first place. They have romantic ideas of coming home to a dog who's excited to see them, or a family dog that watches out for the children. You know, the whole white picket fence and the family dog photo at Christmas. Then they pick a dog that doesn't come close to matching their lifestyle, and before long they're in way over their heads." Netta shook her head.

"What are the other reasons?" I asked.

"Well, disasters—fires, floods, hurricanes. People rarely think about the animals that become homeless and ownerless. It doesn't happen often, thank goodness, but when it does there's work up the yin-yang. 'Scuze my French. If it wasn't for foster parents we wouldn't survive." Netta wiped her forehead like she had just relived an ordeal.

"OK, so if someone wants to foster a puppy, what do they do?" I looked at Cooper hoping at some point he would jump in and say something.

"Call me. I like to meet with them and find out what their expectations are and if I have a dog that's a good fit."

"What's a good fit?" Cooper piped up, almost knocking me off my chair. *Wow! That's actually a good question!*

Netta smiled at Cooper and said, "It depends on several things: how often they're home, where the dog's going to sleep and eat, energy levels—"

"Energy levels?" I interrupted.

"There's nothing worse than having a crazy, hyper dog matched up with someone who works all day or spends most of their time on the computer. The same is true for a laid-back dog that has a foster parent who is always on the go, taking the dog with them everywhere, never still for a moment. People don't really think about these things when they decide to get a puppy." Netta refilled her cup with tea, took a sip, and set it down. "It's my job to make sure this doesn't happen."

"What if it does?" I asked and looked at Cooper, who finally looked like he had a heartbeat.

"Well, the foster dog comes back to the kennel, and we see if we can find a better match." She scooted her chair in closer and leaned her elbows on the table. "If you can't take your dog on a walk at least once a day for thirty minutes, you've no business getting a dog in the first place. I know it sounds harsh, but it's true."

Guilt crept in like a dark shadow as I listened to the foster dog stories. Netta's voice would soften and sometimes cut out altogether if it was an especially sad story. All I could think about was the way I'd pushed Lilly away from me the first day; she must have been terrified. I was relieved that we had a better relationship now. *#goodfriends*

We talked more about breed choices and I sat back, satisfied. This was awesome; we had enough information for a couple of blog posts. Cooper jumped and looked at the time when the cuckoo clock chimed.

"We better get going if we want to catch the two o'clock. We still have a long walk down Netta's driveway to get out to the road," he reminded me.

"Yeah, you're right. We better get going. Netta, this was great. Is it OK if we call or come by again sometime?"

"Of course. I can always use an extra hand. There are dogs to walk, kennels to clean—you name it, we need it. You should bring your dad next time," she said as she stood. "Here, let me pack you up some zucchini cookies for the road. That's the least I can do since I didn't feed you any lunch."

We watched as Netta packed the golden brown cookies with mysterious green stuff poking out. Cooper looked at me and crossed his eyes, and I tried really hard not to laugh.

Cooper and I planned our next blog post during the ride home. One thing we knew for sure: this next post was going to be awesome!

Chapter 13

School had already let out when the bus dropped us off, so it was easy to blend in with the other walkers. Paige hadn't walked with me since the day I'd made her mad, so I didn't worry about running into her. We hadn't gone far when we heard a familiar voice behind us. I whispered to Cooper that BBD was in the building. He looked at me quizzically until he saw me pointing behind us.

"Cooper and Madison, sittin' in a tree, K-I-S-S-I—"

"Shut up, Donald." I whipped around. "You're such a jerk. Why can't you just leave people alone?" I didn't expect an answer, but I glared at him anyway. What I wanted was to put my fist through his mouth.

"*Ooooh*, I'm so scared. Sticking up for your weenie boyfriend?" As Donald got closer, his smile grew bigger and his height towered over both of us.

"You're the weenie. Don't you have anything better to do than get into people's faces? How about you head on over to your cousin Sasha's? I'm sure she's got something for you to do!" Sasha was Donald's cousin who lived one street over. She was two years older than he was, and I'd heard she'd beaten the crap out of him once because he wouldn't give her his baseball mitt. Ever since, Donald has tried to live it down by picking on whoever happens to be in front of him. *I know, low blow, but this is BBD!*

"Whatever, Madison. I know you guys weren't at school today." He rubbed his hands together like an evil villain thinking of horrible things to do to us. "I'm sure Ms. B would like to know where you two lovebirds were. Maybe I should tell her."

"Donald, don't. If you do, you'll be really sorry. I'll tell her you've been taking lunch money from Cooper. I'm sure he isn't the only one, either."

Donald made a strange face at Cooper and cleared his throat. "Oh, settle down. I'm not going to rat you out, but you do owe me." His smile turned up at the corners like a clown waiting to burst from a cannon.

"And what could you possibly want from us?" I could tell he was digging in his brain for something.

"OK, so you know that science project that we're supposed to have done by next Friday?"

"Yeah, what about it?" This was so stupid. I felt as if I was on *iCarly*, trying to get out of trouble after skipping class. *#lameness*

"Well, one of you needs to do my project." Donald folded his arms as if he'd just tied up a present. "But it has to be good—nothing dumb or nerdy."

"Good grief, Donald. You haven't even started it, have you?"

"Make it about recycling. Ms. B likes that stuff."

"Sure, whatever. Come on, Cooper." I was worried about fixing the messages on the answering machine and was anxious to get started. I'd also planned on walking Lilly and work on my own science project. BBD ran ahead and yelled something which neither Cooper nor I could understand.

"He's such an über jerk!" I said.

"I agree." Cooper took his hands out of his pockets where he had put them when Donald arrived. "What was that you called him?"

"It's just a code that Paige and I came up with. BBD; it stands for Big Bad Donald, you know, because he thinks he's *soooo* tough." I had almost forgotten that Paige and I used to have fun coming up with acronyms for people we didn't like. *I miss Paige.*

"That's pretty funny," he said.

"We have to go out to Netta's again. It sounds like a weekend would be perfect because we could stay longer. I just have to figure out how to do it without my dad finding out."

"There might be a way. What about this Saturday we work on the blog over at my house? Would he let you do that?" Cooper tipped his head, waiting for a sign from me that it was OK to go on.

"I guess so; he knows we're working together on it. What are you thinking?" Part of me didn't like the idea of going to his house—not sure where it came from, but maybe it's just that I don't know him very well.

"Well, there's a bus at around nine thirty. If we took it, we'd be out at Netta's by eleven. It would give us a good four hours before we'd have to catch the three o'clock back home." Cooper looked at me and shook his head. "Yeah, it's probably too long to be away, huh?"

The idea was logical in a crazy kind of way. "No, it's not that; I might be able to do it. It's just that Henry likes to spend Saturdays getting things done around the house. Unlike today, he'll be home. Let me think for a minute." Cooper looked at the ground like I'd just punished him, but I just needed to think. "No, you don't understand. My dad is pretty particular about his Saturdays. He has a system and this would definitely not fit, besides the fact that he'd insist on meeting your uncle and taking me there..." *Think, think. How can I make this happen?*

"Maybe we should just stick to Fridays," Cooper said.

"No, there has to be a way. What if you came over a couple of times next week? You know, to 'work on our project.'" I made air quotes. "Henry would get to know you, and maybe it wouldn't be such a big deal for me to go to your place. You're just down the street." This might work. Henry just had to feel comfortable. He'll be glad I'm making new friends.

"I don't know. I'm not good at meeting new people." Cooper shoved his hands back in his pockets and he kicked nervously at the tuft of grass in front of him.

"Yeah, I wouldn't have noticed." I winked. "Come on, Cooper, it wasn't so bad at Netta's once you warmed up," I said, looking into his two pools of blue. *#alert #stomach-weirdness*

"I guess so. When should I come?"

"Monday. You can walk home with me." I looked at my watch, it was going on 5:30pm and I had to beat Henry home before six. "Hey, I really gotta go. See you on Monday, OK?" My feet were almost running.

"Uh-huh, Monday," he said.

I ran all the way home and through the back door, tossed my backpack on the table and started going through the messages. After a couple of hang-ups, I found the message from the school.

"Hello, Mr. Morgan. Madison wasn't at school today, and we wanted to check in to see if she was excused. Please call us at your earliest convenience."

I had to be careful to erase only the one from school. Then I ran through the Caller ID list and found the matching number so I could delete that, too. Henry could never know I'd skipped school. He'd kill me for sure.

A heavy boulder dropped into the pit of my stomach. *#guilt*

Chapter 14

When Dad pulled into the driveway, I'd already opened my laptop. My stomach was queasy, but I focused on the screen even though the words I'd just typed were a blur.

"Hello, Madison. How was your day?" He had a bag of fried chicken and Joes, my favorite; thick cuts of fried potato drenched in a a yummy combination of spices. It's our Friday night tradition—that and watching a movie. Lately we'd seen some pretty lame ones; Dad usually picks them. He keeps bringing home these kiddie movies. Last week we watched "Puppies in Space." Even he thought it was dumb by the time we got to the end.

"Good. How was yours?" I asked. My stomach churned and turned with guilt.

"I had a great day. It isn't often I get to the end of the week and feel as if everything just fell into place, each block right where it needs to be." Henry relates everything to building. *Hello? He* is *an architect.*

"So, what's the movie tonight?" I smiled back, relieved he was in a good mood. *#relief*

"I think you'll like this one. It's the last *Harry Potter* that we didn't get to see in the theater." Dad sat his things on the counter and slipped off his jacket. Maybe this weekend wouldn't be so bad after all.

***

My body jolted. I had been reaching for the dog in the red tub again. Same dream as always, same dog. I tried to pull my brain back to the real world. It was just a dream.

What time was it? I flipped my alarm clock around so I could see the face, and bright green numbers seared into my tired eyes. Five a.m. It was pointless to even try to go back to sleep; my mind was too awake and full of frantic business.

I thought of my mother's box hidden under my bed and reached down and pulled it out. This was the first time I'd looked at it since Dad had given it to me. I sucked in a deep breath and slowly lifted the lid.

At the top was a roll of newspaper wrapped with a rubber band. I ran my finger underneath the brittle rubber band and it snapped apart. The roll opened and the newspaper clippings that had been fastened tightly for so long held their curl. There were pictures of dogs and some of my mother and Netta. I tried to be gentle as I pulled each clipping apart and laid it out on my bed. Headlines blared out at me: "Rescued," "Homes for Homeless Dogs."

One headline immediately grabbed my attention, and I pulled it closer. The headline read, "Hurricane Katrina's Lost

Animals Find Refuge." The accompanying picture showed a river of water where rooftops poked out just above the current. I stared at the photo. At the center, floating in the waves, was a large, red tub. Inside sat a dog. His eyes were sharp with fear and trained intently on the photographer. His fox-like muzzle pointed in the air, no doubt catching scents of everything around him. *I've seen this before. It isn't just a bad dream!*

Under the picture the caption read, "Stuck in the tub for almost three days." Then the first paragraph said, "Thanks to the women of Second Chance Dog Shelter, Dakota not only found dry land and a warm place to stay but was eventually reunited with his family."

I stared at the clipping. The tub wasn't a dream and neither was the dog. I'd seen this before, and that was why it filled my dreams. *Why did Dad keep this from me?*

My dreams and my desire for a dog made sense now. Even better, for the first time I realized that my strange obsession was really a gift—a special bond between my mother and me. Magically the sun peeked through the slits in the blinds and cast thin ribbons of light across the bed. Morning had finally arrived and with it a new sense of purpose.

Chapter 15

"Don't forget to walk Lilly before you guys get busy on your blog. I should be home by five p.m., and we could do hot dogs and beans for dinner."

Monday had finally arrived, and Cooper was coming home with me after school. When we have guests, Dad likes to get out the barbecue and fire it up to cook hot dogs. And there's his secret recipe for beans. I know it's just ketchup and brown sugar, but he still insists on calling them his "special beans."

Paige was at our meeting place in the morning. She hadn't walked with me since our big blowout last week. I was actually glad to see her; I'd missed her. And then it hit me—she knew. She'd found out about Friday, probably from Donald, and now she was going to ask for the details. Even so, I was glad to see her.

"I'm still mad at you, Madison Morgan, but I don't want to walk alone, and Mom couldn't give me a ride," she said and set a quick pace down the street.

"Well, I'm still mad, too...but I'm glad to see you." I hardly remembered what we'd been mad about, but I didn't want to give in too easily. We walked along in silence for a while. The sidewalk was wet from the rain during the night, and there were little puddles to skip over, which we would have done if we were still in grade school. Paige broke the silence first.

"My mom and dad are getting a divorce." She said it so plainly I wasn't sure what I should say.

"That sucks. I'm sorry." I struggled to choose the right words. "Do you want to talk about it?"

"Not really. I just wanted you to know," she said and kicked a loose rock.

"Well, if you want to talk..." I put my hand on her shoulder and she crumpled, turned to me, and started to sob into my shoulder. I hugged her and patted her back.

"I know...you don't have your mom...so you probably think it's silly, but I feel like I'm losing both my parents."

"No, I don't at all. It's probably confusing," I said.

"That's it. I feel like my head is spinning and my life's falling apart."

Paige was usually dramatic, but this didn't seem like drama. She was really upset. Part of me wanted to ask her where her new popular friends were and why wasn't she talking to them, but I didn't.

"I'm sorry; that must really hurt," I said instead.

"Yeah…it does. Thanks, Madison." We didn't talk the rest of the way to school, and when we got there she ran ahead to catch up with Katie and her other friends. I wanted to be mad, but I couldn't. Maybe being with them would help her forget about it, at least when she was at school. That didn't make it hurt my feelings any less.

***

That afternoon Cooper walked home with me. We took Lilly for a walk, and she still acted scared of him, tucking her tail between her legs. By the time the walk was over, she seemed to have chilled out and even let Cooper pat her on the head. She'd accepted him and I could feel her calmness.

We were starving when Henry came through the door at five o'clock. He told us to set the table and pull the condiments out of the fridge.

"Cooper, want to head out to the patio and help me get the barbecue going?" Cooper looked at me, and I nodded my head. I felt funny that Dad was getting all chummy with him.

I watched from the window; Cooper was nodding yes and no, and I knew my dad was giving him the Henry-test. He likes to ask a lot of questions when he's getting to know a new friend of mine. I'm sure Cooper was thrilled. I remembered when Paige came over for the first time, he asked her all sorts of things about her family, her hobbies, and where she lived. Cooper looked to be handling it OK, even though his hands were in his pockets. I headed out with the hot dogs to save him.

"Cooper was telling me you guys already have your blog online?"

"Yeah, it went live on Friday. I told you that." Henry likes to make the person he just grilled feel as if he's uncovered important information. I'm not sure why, but it always makes me feel like I was hiding something from him, and since this time I really was hiding the fact that Cooper and I had gone to Netta's, my discomfort was magnified.

"Here, Cooper. Why don't you take the tongs and turn the hot dogs over?" Another technique Henry uses to make people feel like they belong: he assigns tasks, and then they're members of the family. He has a way of setting people at ease. Like when you get on an elevator with a bunch of people you don't know and it's all hard and awkward. Henry just starts talking and by the time we get to our destination, five floors up, they're making dinner plans. OK, maybe not that comfortable, but somehow he pushes the stiff, tense air out and everyone relaxes. I like that. It even makes me proud that he's my dad. *#coolestdadever*

"I don't know, Mr. Morgan. I haven't ever cooked on a barbecue before."

"Ah, go ahead. It's not that big a deal," I said.

"Madison, you're right that it isn't hard, but that doesn't mean it isn't important."

"Right, Dad. I'm sure Cooper's thrilled to have the opportunity to turn our weenies." Everyone laughed. Cooper took the tongs and turned the hot dogs. Lilly put her nose in the air and perched herself right beside the grill. I could feel her anxious appetite and my stomach growled. Dad poked one of the hotdogs with a fork and tossed it out into the yard. We all watched as Lilly scrambled after the bouncing hot dog and then caught it, her front paws on top and took a bite off the end.

When the dogs were the perfect shade of black, I'd carefully explained to Cooper how much better they tasted that way, he put them on the serving plate and we headed to the table. The look on Cooper's face told me he wasn't convinced about their burned exterior tasting yummy. The beans had been on the stove and were wafting a sweet aroma that made my stomach growl. We spent the rest of the meal talking about Lilly and our next blog post.

Chapter 16

Cooper and I sat in the back of the classroom on Wednesday after school and worked on details for our blog. Ms. B had gone to a meeting and said she'd be back in an hour to help us post.

"So, have you asked your dad about Saturday yet?" Cooper asked.

"No, I just haven't found the right time. Tonight I'll explain that we're going to take pictures at your place and you can't bring the camera over to my house, and that's why we have to go to yours on Saturday." I was pretty pleased with my explanation and had no reason to think that Henry wouldn't go for it.

"So, what do you want to post about this time?" Cooper said as he placed elbow on the desk and his chin in his hand. "We have too much information for just one post, don't you think?"

"Yeah, I think you're right. We need to split up the information somehow. Maybe this post can be more about where the dogs come from and what people like Netta do."

"That's good, and then the next one could be more about the foster dog stuff." His blue eyes twinkled; it was a look I was seeing more often. I also noticed that he wore a clean T-shirt— orange, for a change—and he'd even tucked it in.

"OK, I'll write the part about where the dogs come from, and you work on what shelters like Netta's do," I said. He nodded and got right to work, so I did, too. Maybe I wouldn't have to do all the work after all.

> Have you ever wondered where the dogs that no one wants end up? If they're lucky they find their way to a rescue shelter, with the help of people who care. There are several shelters across the country, but they can't keep up with the number of homeless dogs. Many of them run on very tight budgets, and most are funded by donations. Second Chance Shelter is one that works hard to find homes for dogs like Lilly.

By the time Ms. B came back, we had rewritten the post and just needed her to check it. After she showed us a few things we'd missed—a word or two misspelled and a couple of periods—we posted the second entry to the blog. The blog said we'd had at least one hundred views but no comments. We hoped that the new post would bring at least one comment.

***

When we got to my house, Lilly was waiting at the door with her leash in her mouth. We laughed, clipped the leash to her collar, and headed down the street and rounded the corner on Stuart. Cooper stopped and crouched down to pet Lilly.

"I have to ask: why do you call your dad Henry all the time?"

"I don't all the time. It's just he came into my life when I was three, and it took me a while to learn to say Henry correctly, so when he and Mom married, it didn't seem like a big deal. Henry always says it's just a name." Cooper shrugged and Lilly pulled, so we continued down the sidewalk.

We'd only gone by few houses when BBD walked out from between a small, white ranch style house and a green two story. *Great, just what we need!*

"So Donald," I asked, "what has you out slithering and sneaking between houses?" I hoped to catch him off guard by speaking first.

"None of your business, lovebirds," BBD said with a smirk.

"We're not lovebirds," Cooper said a little too guiltily, even I thought so.

"Yeah, I think the bigger question is why you're coming out on Stuart. Your house is clear over on Bingham. Up to no good, I bet."

BBD looked at Cooper and then back at me. "I could ask you the same question. What are you two doing?" His tone sounded like he was actually interested and not just giving us a hard time.

"Isn't it obvious? We're walking a dog."

Good one, Cooper. I was surprised; Cooper was looking straight at Donald. They both stood their ground, staring for a moment, and then surprisingly, Donald looked away.

"Yeah, yeah, all right, I get it. Don't get uptight. I've got to get going anyway; I don't have time to deal with you two," he said. *Deal with us? What does that mean?* BBD walked in the opposite direction.

"Wow, Cooper. Where did that come from?"

"What? Where did what come from?" He looked at me as if I'd offended him.

"Whoa." I put up my hands. "I'm just saying that I've never seen you stand up to the BBD before."

"I don't know; it was different this time. I think we finally have an agreement," he said.

"What kind of agreement?"

"Let's just say he isn't holding all the cards anymore."

I watched BBD disappear and wondered where he was headed. It bugged me that they had something between them that I didn't know about, but Cooper had already run ahead with Lilly so I couldn't try to get it out of him.

We finished Lilly's walk then went back to my house and fed her. "Are you hungry?" I asked.

"*Mmm*, I guess so."

"Well, we have popcorn, graham crackers, or fruit. Those are the only things in Henry's system."

"What do you mean system?" he asked.

"OK, this is the deal: if we're going to hang out, you have to understand a few things about Henry." I pulled out a chair, sat down at the table, and nodded my head for him to take the other chair.

"So, what's the system?" Cooper folded his arms and waited for an answer.

"It's how he deals with the fact that my mom is gone. He says it helps him manage everything without feeling crazy." To tell the truth, I hadn't really thought about the why until now, it just was. Now that I had to explain it to someone else it made perfect sense. "I guess it's his way of staying in control and taking care of me."

"Does the system ever change?"

"Not very often; that's the problem. He made his system when I was five. It worked then, but now I'm almost twelve and there are some things about it that are pretty lame. Like the other morning when I wanted to empty the dishwasher after dinner instead of before. I was so annoyed when he explained why we have a system in the first place.

"There isn't anything really wrong with the system. It's just that it's his system—not mine—and sometimes I just want to do things my way."

"Is that when your mother died? When you were five?" Cooper's eyes rested on me and I felt warm and tingly. *#weirdness*

"Yeah. I hardly remember her but sometimes if I close my eyes and think about her, I can see her; but as soon as my mind wanders, she's gone like a puff of smoke. What about you?" I changed the subject. "How come you live with your uncle? Where are your parents?"

"My dad—well, nobody knows where he is, and when I turned nine my mom thought that it would be good for me to live with my uncle for a while. I think she was having a hard time providing for me since she was always losing her job. The strange thing is, after about six months she stopped calling every day, then it was once a month, and now it's been almost four months and I haven't heard from her at all."

"That must be tough," I said.

"I just try not to think about it too much." He shrugged his shoulders.

"Yeah, me too. Sometimes it's just easier not to think about her."

"The hardest part is we move around a lot. I hate it. Never in one place long enough to make any friends. If it happens again, I think I'm gonna jump on a bus." Cooper looked really depressed so I decided to change the subject.

"Well, let's get working on that blog schedule thing." We worked on the blog for the rest of the afternoon. Ms. B had asked us to come up with a schedule so people would know when and what we were going to post.

Blog Schedule

Monday: Foster Dog, Lilly. The journal of being a foster dog parent.

Tuesday: Breed Characteristics. Researching different breeds.

Wednesday: Foster Dog, Lilly. Funny things Lilly does.

Thursday: Training Tips. Simple tips about training your dog.

Friday: Adoption Friday. Pictures of dogs to adopt and contact information.

Chapter 17

"Madison, have you finished your homework?" Henry yelled up the stairs.

"Just about," I said, looking at the stack of books next to my desk. "I only have math left." *#lies. I'm getting way too good at this.*

"OK. I've got to go out for a while. I'll be back in...say an hour."

"Sure, Dad. I'll be here." Just enough time to call Netta and ask her a couple of questions. When I heard the car pull out of the garage, I dug out the phone number from my coat pocket, ran down the stairs, and stopped at the bottom. *Darn, I need my notebook and pen. #duh*

When I got back downstairs, I dialed the phone and sat down at the table. After three rings, Netta answered. "Hello, Second Chance Dog Shelter, this is Netta."

"Hi, Netta, this is Madison," I said. Lilly walked in quietly and curled up at my feet.

After a short pause Netta said, "What's up, Madison? How is Lilly doing?"

"Great. Lilly is doing fine." Lilly's ears perked up. I opened my notebook to the questions I'd scribbled during history.

"I have some questions for you—you know, for the blog?" I hoped she'd remember.

"Oh, sure...sure, ask away." I thought I would start with the easy ones and then slip one in about my mom. Maybe she wouldn't have time to stop her answer before it bubbled out. I asked her about the process someone would need to go through to adopt a foster dog, how long the average stay was, and what the costs were.

"All medical is provided for the dog. Foster parents need only provide the home and food," she answered.

"How many dogs do you have at one time?"

"It depends but right now I am full up. All twenty-five of my kennels are occupied." She took a loud tired sigh.

OK, here goes.

"So Netta, when my mom and you started the rescue shelter, did she do anything special for the dogs?" I didn't know how else to ask. Any way it came out would be weird.

"I'm not sure I know what you mean," Netta said and cleared her throat. "Special, like what?"

"Oh, I don't know. Did she do stuff with the dogs like train them?" I was totally beating around the bush, but I just didn't know how to explain it. *How do you ask someone if your mother could read dogs' minds? #complicated*

"Oh, for sure. Your mom was gifted that way—always spending time rehabilitating the worst off." Netta paused.

"What do you mean gifted?" *Now we were getting somewhere.*

"You know, Madison, this is something you should be talking to your dad about. I don't feel comfortable doing it." *Here it comes, the let's-talk-about-it-later excuse.*

"Netta, please. Dad won't talk about her." I tore out a sheet of paper from the notebook and started wadding it in my hand. "You're the only person I can talk to about this. It's driving me crazy." I felt a lump growing in my throat.

"OK, OK...let's see. Well, by gifted I mean she had a way with the dogs. They appeared to listen to her even when she wasn't speaking to them, like she could not only see into their minds, but she could communicate with them mentally. I asked about it once, and she said it wasn't words but something else. She wasn't even sure what it was, but she said it was like emotional energy." Netta stopped and cleared her throat. "Please don't tell your father I told you this. He never understood it or her need to use her gift, especially near the end."

"I won't, I promise. Dad's going to be home in a minute, so I need to get off the phone," I said, staring out the window.

"This is a difficult subject for him, and the last thing I wanna do is step on his toes or make him angry. This is something you should talk to him about."

"Why? Would he be angry? Who would he be angry with?" This just wasn't making any sense.

"Me, Madison. That's why he doesn't want you around me and why you never come out to visit," Netta said. "I've already said too much."

"OK, I understand. Well, not really, but OK. Thanks for talking to me."

Chapter 18

Dad had a morning conference call with a contractor on Saturday, which made it easier for me to leave. Cooper and I had decided to meet halfway since we had to walk back over to Hawthorne to catch the bus. Lilly whined when I picked up my backpack and headed for the door. I reached down, petted her, and told her I would be back.

There was a flutter in my stomach when I thought about seeing Cooper, but I decided I was just excited to be heading out to Netta's again. I had so many questions and hoped she would answer them. I still hadn't figured out what I was going to tell her about Dad. She wouldn't approve of my sneaking around behind his back, so I had to make sure she believed that Dad let me ride all the way out to her place with Cooper. *#biggerlie #tooeasy*

Cooper was already waiting by the time I reached our meeting spot. He wore a clean T-shirt, and it looked like he had actually found his long lost hairbrush. *He doesn't look half bad; almost cute—well, that is, if I cared.*

We walked quickly toward the school to the bus stop. Just as we arrived, we heard heavy footsteps running toward us and we turned to see Donald panting laboriously. When he caught up to us, he bent over, put his hands on his knees, and sucked in a loud breath.

"*Whew!* I didn't think I was going to make it!" he breathed out deeply.

"Make it to what?" I asked.

"The bus, stupid. Isn't that why we're here?" The BBD quickly caught his breath.

"And if it were, what's it to you?" I crossed my arms.

"Well, I'm going with you," he said and looked at Cooper, who glared right back at him.

"Yeah right! When dogs blog," I retorted.

"Why would you want to come with us?" Cooper asked, glancing at me and then back at Donald.

"Because I know your secret, and if you don't want anyone to know where you're going, you're going to have to take me with you." He folded his arms smugly and leaned in toward Cooper, as if I wasn't even there.

"Wait—you can't. Netta isn't expecting you," I said. She wasn't expecting us, either, but he didn't have to know that. "And besides, you wouldn't want to go. You don't like dogs, except of course to tease and torture them."

"That's not true," he said louder than was necessary. "Someone has to keep you two out of trouble."

"I think this is a bad idea, Donald." Cooper slid his hands into his pockets and took a step back.

"Well, of course, but you don't have a choice, do you?" Donald looked back at me. "You don't want me talking, do you?"

It looked like he was right; there really wasn't a choice. Cooper cringed like a rabbit backing away from a hungry wolf.

"Fine. You know that we're going out there to help with cleaning kennels and walking dogs, right?" I made one last effort to discourage him.

"Where is the kennel, anyway?" He rubbed his hands together as if things were working just like he planned.

"We are going out to the Second Chance Dog Shelter on Highway 17 to work, get it? *Work*," Cooper snapped. Then he did something so awesome it was difficult to believe my eyes. He pressed his hand in the middle of Donald's hefty chest and pushed—not hard, but enough for BBD to lose his balance a bit. When he regained his stance, he squinted at Cooper who squinted back.

"Yeah, work, Donald. Have you heard of it?" I looked at him like I thought he was an idiot, which I did. "If you think we're still going to help you with your science project, you better think again."

"OK, you two, stop ganging up on me. You might be glad to have another person in case something happens." He placed his hands on his hips and held his chin high.

"Oh, now you're our superhero? Geez, you really are full of yourself," I said as the bus pulled up. "You better have your own fare, 'cause we aren't paying it."

"I don't need a fare because I have something better." He reached into his jacket pocket. "A bus pass. Tada!" I had to admit that did surprise me. He went on to brag that he takes the bus all the time, sometimes all the way into Seattle.

The bus ride was long and quiet except for the muffled sound of someone's iPod and the creaking of the bus seats whenever we hit a bump. Cooper had leaned his head against the window and was asleep, Donald stared out the window, and I was staring at both of them. It was obvious that something was different between them, but I didn't know what it was. This had to be the weirdest group of misfits ever, yet there was something calming about the fact that we were together and headed to the same destination. I can't figure out what Donald's deal is and that makes me uneasy, but at the same time he looks harmless watching the telephone poles whiz past.

***

"Be careful, Maddy," Henry said, giving Mom a look that said he wasn't sure this was a good idea.

"Henry, she'll be fine. I'm right here." Mom crouched beside me as we peeked into the stall where a shiny black Lab drummed his tail happily on the kennel floor. "Maddy, this is Razor."

I could hear other dogs in the kennel. Some were jumping and carrying on, while others were simply circling their kennels with an occasional bark tossed into the air. Razor's piercing dark eyes met mine. There was sadness in them, but also relief.

"Mom, why is Razor sad?" I asked.

"Razor was just rescued from a bad place where someone didn't treat him very nicely," Mom said.

Dad reached down and set his hand on Mom's shoulder. "Come on Rachel, we need to get going."

"Oh, Henry, we'll be there in plenty of time," Mom said, standing up and brushing off her knees. "Stop being so uptight."

***

"Madison…Madison, wake up." Cooper shook my arm. "We're here; time to get off the bus."

I must have dozed off. My mother's voice still echoed in my head.

Chapter 19

"Well, this is the middle of nowhere," Donald said when we jumped off the bus. It was true; there wasn't a house in sight. Tall fir trees lined the sides of the gravel driveway.

"Why'd we get off here?" Donald asked looking around cautiously.

"'Cause this is where the rescue shelter is. Duh," I said, heading down the road.

"Yeah, you're the one that wanted to come," Cooper said following me.

"*Oooh*, a little touchy, Cooper. I just meant that this is really out in the sticks." Donald followed. "What are we going to do here, again?"

"We're going to work in the kennels with the dogs," Cooper said picking up the pace down the long driveway.

"And you better not get in the way or mess this up by doing something stupid." I shouted over my shoulder trying to keep up. I knew Donald; he was always looking for ways to ruin a perfectly great day.

The kennel was just ahead, and we could hear barking inside. Netta said she was full to capacity with about twenty-five dogs right now, so I expected the barking. What I didn't expect was the rush of emotion that flooded over me when I opened the door. My hands started to sweat like they had that day with Lilly, and my heart beat faster. Something fluttered deep in my stomach like when I'm in a large group of people I don't know. Then it was like everything in my brain went black, and I saw images flash like a camera rapidly taking pictures. I saw human feet, dog hair, and canine eyes. The images were a jumble of pieces held together by a string of emotions—sad, happy, and excited—and they changed almost faster than I could process.

I stepped over the threshold and into the first row of kennels, and then I steadied myself against the wall. After I took a deep breath and tried to relax, the barking quieted. When I knelt down to look at the first little dog, the barking stopped altogether. My hands stopped sweating, I wasn't nervous anymore, and my heart slowed to a normal rate. Then I walked in and out of the rows of kennels and found that all the dogs were sitting and waiting for something. It seemed like they were waiting for me to do something, but I had no idea what I was supposed to do. Cooper and Donald stayed by the door, their faces scrunched in puzzlement.

"Hey, Madison, is that you?" Netta's voice echoed against the cement walls.

"Yeah, over here in C row," I said as I stood up and walked in her direction. The quiet that fell over all the dogs was eerie, but calm at the same time. *What the heck was all that about?*

"I only know one person who could calm a kennel full of dogs. She had a way about her. I never figured out what exactly was going on, but there was no doubt your mother had a gift." Netta handed me a bag of kibble and directed me to fill each dish and slide it under each kennel's gate. Netta went and grabbed the hose and showed Cooper how to fill the water troughs through the bars.

"So what's your name?" she asked Donald.

"Donald."

"Are you here to help or watch?" Netta's matter-of-fact tone caught Donald off guard.

"A...well, help I guess," he said. All I'd ever seen Donald do was tease dogs; I wasn't sure he was capable of anything else.

"Good. I need someone to drag that bale of hay over here. You and I will clear out the kennels and lay new straw."

I smiled at Cooper. Something about Donald cleaning dog poop seemed fitting.

"I don't think I want to get into the kennels," he said. I'd never seen that look on his face. It was definitely fear. *Seriously?*

"What's the matter, Donald? Are you scared?" I know it was mean, but after everything he'd done I thought he deserved to be teased.

"Donald will do fine, right?" Netta dismissed my comment. *Yeah, I get it.* Now I felt like the jerk.

"Yeah, I'm gonna do fine. Where's that bale of hay?"

***

After an hour or so, we had all finished our tasks. Netta took a deep breath and said, "Wow, that would have taken me most of the day to do all that. Thanks so much!"

"So where do all the dogs come from?" Donald asked.

"Lots of places...it depends. Sometimes someone will call and say they can't have a dog in their new apartment and need to find a home for it. Other times I get a phone call from somebody who has found an injured or abandoned dog, and I go retrieve them."

"What happens when there's no more room? Like now—aren't you full?" I asked.

"Then it gets tricky. I have two dependable foster homes that are sometimes willing to take an extra dog or two. Then I have to start calling other rescue shelters and see if they have room. It can get really complicated when there's a long distance involved. The good thing is, ever since Hurricane Katrina the network has grown, and we are more connected across the country. That is something your mother would be proud of."

"Why?" I asked.

"Oh, your mom was instrumental in coordinating the rescue of animals during the Katrina cleanup. She was amazing." Netta smiled and nodded.

"Dad's never said anything about that."

"Well, it was a tough time, and they didn't see eye to eye on the whole rescue thing. He thought she should have stayed home and rested, but that wasn't who she was. Rachel was always about action. She was spontaneous and that drove Henry crazy." Netta stopped and shook her head. "I'm sorry. I'm sure he'll tell you when he's ready."

"Um, I was wondering—" Cooper said trying to fill the uncomfortable silence and change the subject. *Not so fast.*

"Did my mom come here often, Netta?" I asked.

"All the time…well, as often as Henry…would let her, especially at the end." Netta bit her lip. "So what else do you need for your blog?"

"We could use some pictures. Would it be OK if I took some?" Cooper interjected.

"Sure," Netta said adjusting her pink bandana.

"I was thinking of showing some of the dogs in the kennel and—"

"Oh…of course," Netta nodded her head and then looked at me. "Why don't you and Donald get started, and Madison and I will head up to the house." I gave both Donald and Cooper a stay-out-of-trouble look.

"Come on, Cooper." Donald grabbed Cooper's camera off my shoulder. I glared at him, but he didn't pay me any attention. Netta and I headed for the house.

Chapter 20

"I'm sorry to ask you all these questions. It's so frustrating. Dad gave me Mom's tin box—the one with the clippings in it—but he still won't talk about her."

Netta reached for the door, and we walked into the overstuffed mudroom. There were enough coats, hats, and boots to clothe an entire school. We slipped off our shoes, and then she put a kettle on the stove and pulled out a plate of cookies. I sat at the table.

"Look, Madison, Henry loved your mother very much. We all did. The last few months were really tough; Rachel was so sick, but she wouldn't stop working...she said if she stopped then she might as well die. She really felt that it was the dogs that kept her going as long as she did, and Henry just couldn't see it. He wanted her to stay home and rest; he believed she would have lived longer if she'd rested." Netta's watery eyes spilled tears onto her plump, doughy cheeks, and she quickly wiped them with the back of her hand. "If this is hard for me, it must be triply hard for Henry."

"I know. I don't want to hurt him, but she was my mother and I need to know who she was. What was important to her—"

A loud shriek pierced my ears, and Netta jumped up and headed for the door. I followed her out, stumbling over the step as I struggled to put my shoes back on.

When we got to the kennels, Donald and Cooper were just coming out the door with their hands over their ears, dripping wet.

"What happened?" I yelled over the screeching alarm.

"I don't know. You stay here; I'll check it out." Netta plunged into the building. Even after the alarm stopped, it echoed in my brain along with the frightened dog howls. Cooper and Donald were out of breath. Donald had a red welt on his cheek, and Cooper had one on his arm.

"What the heck happened in there?" I screamed, and then I realized I was talking louder then I needed to, now that the alarm was off. When Netta came out, her hair and bandana were plastered against her head and her clothes were dripping.

"That was the fire alarm," Netta said. We heard sirens getting closer, and then the fire truck barreled to a stop right in front of us.

"Netta, what's going on?" The firefighter towered over her.

"I'm not sure," she said looking to the boys for an explanation.

"I don't know. All of a sudden water was squirting everywhere, and the alarm was screeching and the dogs were barking." Cooper took a breath, put his hands on his knees, and bent over.

I looked over at Donald who was now kicking the dirt as if we were just standing around shooting the breeze. I knew it; he just couldn't stay out of trouble.

"So help me, Donald, what did you do?" I went for him and pushed him up against the door.

"Wait, wait! Don't look at me like that. It wasn't my fault." He moved me back away from him.

"It was, too," Cooper said lunging toward Donald, his T-shirt stuck to his body, ribs visible.

"OK, kids, let's just settle down. We'll figure it out," the firefighter said, pushing through us to the door. When the door opened, the barking wafted out along with the sour smell of wet dog hair. I felt my stomach tighten, and my breathing increased so I had to open my mouth to get enough air.

Cooper looked at me. "Are you OK, Madison?"

"I don't know. I feel really strange." I leaned up against the building and slid down until I was sitting in the dirt. Netta sat beside me and rubbed my back. The flashes of frightened dogs and water sped before my eyes. I wanted to tell her, but when I opened my mouth, I realized that I didn't know how to explain it.

"It will be OK; just try to breathe in and out slowly."

Donald had stepped away from us and was looking down the road. It wouldn't surprise me if he just took off running. It would be just like him to skip out when things got sticky.

"It was Donald. He wouldn't stop bugging this one dog. He said he was just trying to get its attention, but he kept sticking the broom handle through the bars. He said he was going to tell. It made me so mad, and he wouldn't stop so I grabbed him. He swung around and whacked my arm with the broom. I grabbed a wet towel off the floor and whopped the side of his face, and he turned and the broom must have hit the sprinkler head. Water sprayed everywhere and that set off the other sprinklers and the alarm." Cooper took a breath and then sighed. "I'm sorry, Madison, I shouldn't have—"

"Shouldn't have what?" Part of me wanted to know but I couldn't really concentrate.

"Oh...you know, everything."

"I don't want to talk about it right now." My breathing was returning to normal, but my mind was a million miles away. The flashing images slowed. One white image remained: a large wolf with blurred edges. It seemed to be waiting. Its gentle eyes watched me, and the more I focused on it the calmer I became.

Netta had gone over to Donald, who was shaking his head and mumbling something about fault. She patted him on the back.

"Good news," the tall firefighter said as he came out the door. "The sprinkler head was just knocked off. We've shut off the main and will replace the head. Everything should be good as new." Netta looked relieved and shook the fireman's hand.

"All except for the mess that these fine gentlemen will be helping me to clean up. Right, boys?"

Both Cooper and Donald nodded, glaring at each other.

"Better get started if you want to finish in time to catch your bus." Netta propped open the door so the stale, wet air could escape and headed in with Cooper and Donald right behind her.

I couldn't move and waved them on. When they emerged about thirty minutes later I'd finally regained my strength but still felt groggy. We only had a few minutes to make it to the bus. Cooper ran ahead, and Donald fell into step with me. Then he leaned in and whispered, "Cooper has a secret—the kind that changes things."

We barely made it to the bus on time and sat silently all the way home. I was so angry with both of them. I stared out the window and thought about the weird way my body took over, the strange flashes in my mind, and finally the wolf—because somehow I knew that was what it was. It lingered there in my vision, watching with soft eyes until my heart had slowed and calm had settled over me like a warm blanket.

When we arrived at our stop, I was still too angry to talk to either of them, so I got off the bus and headed down the road without even saying good-bye. I was pretty sure Netta wouldn't be inviting us out to "help" her anytime soon.

Chapter 21

I went out of my way to avoid both Cooper and Donald during the next week at school. I was really mad at both of them and they knew it. Donald didn't even try to make eye contact with me, and he was ignoring Cooper, which was a vast improvement over being hassled every day by the BBD. What Donald said about Cooper having the kind of secret that changes things nagged at my brain. I'd thought about it all week—that and Cooper's reaction when he'd thought I'd gone down his driveway the day I walked Lilly past his house.

I decided it was time to figure out what was going on at Cooper's house. Ever since I'd heard those dogs and the strange way he had acted, I'd wondered what was really going on there. If Paige and I were still friends, I wouldn't have to do this alone. We used to spy on all the neighbors and pretend they had secret lives that we might expose. Now she's only interested in fashion and who said what to whom. The last time we spoke she'd told me, "You just don't get it." We just don't speak the same language anymore. I was wrong; I would have to do this alone.

All alone.

The next afternoon I waited until the sun was low in the sky and cast shadows so I could get past the front of Cooper's house without someone seeing me. I'd told Henry that I had to give Cooper his missing assignments, and when he asked why I wasn't taking Lilly, I said that it would be easier not to have her with me.

My stomach took a flop and I gritted my teeth. First, I decided I would casually walk by to case the place. I'd seen it on detective shows, and it seemed like a good idea. The house sat back from the road, and one side of the yard had tall poplars that ran down the gravel driveway and circled toward the back of the house. They cast long, tall shadows across the property.

The front porch was stacked with old newspapers and boxes on one side and lawn chairs on the other. Six steps led up to the front door. The green paint was worn around the brass door handle. The house was dark as far as I could see; maybe no one was home. That would certainly make creeping around a lot easier.

I'd spent the afternoon concocting a story about why I was there for in case I got caught. Cooper had missed a couple days of school since our trip to Netta's. I'd say that I brought him some homework from Ms. B. That's why I was carrying this dumb manila folder with papers inside—they were blank of course, but from what Cooper had said I didn't imagine his uncle would have the least bit of interest in his homework. I hoped Cooper would understand that I was just concerned about him and made up the Ms. B story so I wouldn't look stupid.

I stood below the stairs and listened for anyone moving around inside. Then I climbed the rickety steps to the door, put my ear against it, and heard nothing. I glanced around just to be sure no one was around and then shot to the side of the house. The overgrown rhododendron bushes climbed the siding, and I crept along the edge of them, shadowed by the trees. I tripped over a hose but caught myself and luckily didn't make any noise. My heart was beating so fast I could feel it in my throat and could hardly swallow. The German Shepherd guard dogs, tethered tightly to a thick post, strained against their collars and barked. When the ruckus didn't coax anyone outdoors, I relaxed a little bit.

I peered around the last bush, scanned the yard, and heard more barking farther back in the yard. Halfway back there was a faded gray fence that divided the backyard; the barking was coming from behind it. I kept walking and looked over my shoulder every three steps; all the windows were still black and there was only a truck sitting at the end of the driveway. By the amount of rust around the tire rims, and the fact that the hood was up, it probably hadn't moved from that spot in a while.

When I got around the fence, sparse grass covered dried ridges of mud that crunched under my feet. The barking was louder, and the higher pitch pierced my ears. I also heard the sound of puppies whining and the clank of metal.

My stomach tightened and my chest felt like someone was standing on it. There was a small shed blocking my view. My breath tried to keep up with the pounding of my heart.

I wasn't prepared for what I saw next. My jaw must have hit the ground, but I pulled it shut so fast I almost bit my tongue. The cages were stacked four high and six across, each cage probably only three feet by four feet. In each cage were at least two or three dogs, and most had more. There were cages that held only one dog, and some of those had puppies. Those cages were lined with cardboard and newspaper, but it was obvious that the paper hadn't been changed in a long time. The stench rose in a thick cloud of heavy air.

In one cage a small, blackish-brown dog lay on its side. It looked a lot like Lilly, but so thin its bones showed through its skin. She didn't move when I got closer, and her small muzzle was wrapped in bloody gauze. The crusted hair surrounding her eyes told me the poor thing had been crying for days. Her face was made up of matted hair and expressionless eyes that looked like black stones.

All the dogs looked starved. Everywhere I looked there were flies and poop. I'd seen something this horrible only once before: the show Henry and I had watched about puppy mills. I wondered how long this had been here and why nobody had ever discovered it. Is this what Donald was talking about? Why would he care? I've never seen him treat any living thing kindly.

I walked slowly and looked at the overcrowded cages. Sad, cloudy eyes peered from behind grime and knotted hair, and tender paws balanced on thin wire. Some were bleeding and probably infected since they were standing in their own waste, and flies and fleas swarmed around their tiny puppy eyes and noses. Something grabbed my heart and squeezed. I turned and fell against the cages, rattling them so the dogs all started barking louder, all except one. The little dog had no voice, just a raspy whisper.

I balanced around the next corner of cages and doubled over, retched, then sat down hard on a patch of grass. Tears blurred my vision, I trembled, and my fists clenched. I wanted to scream but then remembered where I was. I fumbled for my phone; it wasn't in any of my pockets. I looked around to see if I'd dropped it. *Oh, no, I left it on the table at home.* I knew I had to get out of here, fast.

I stood up, bracing myself against the wall of cages. I'd only taken a few steps when I heard a truck rumbling down the gravel driveway. I dove into the tall grass that was growing underneath the bottom row of cages. I realized where I was when the ammonia hit my nose; dog urine saturated the soft, damp ground. It was difficult to breathe and my eyes stung, but I held still.

"Cooper! Cooper!" someone yelled. His voice sounded anxious and angry. "That boy is never around when I need him." He went around the back of his blue pickup and started pulling out empty wire cages and dropping them on the ground.

My heart had made its way to the top of my chest, and I could hear it beating in my ears. I looked around for an escape route but couldn't see anywhere that wouldn't draw attention. I was grateful the dogs had quieted down; the loud voice must have frightened them into silence.

A screen door creaked open from the back of the house and someone yelled, "There's a buyer on the phone; ya wanna take it?"

"Yeah. You come unload the truck," said a large man dressed in faded blue jeans and a red T-shirt that bulged just above a huge brass buckle.

The boy's voice was whiny and dripped with contempt. "Isn't that Cooper's job? Why do I—?"

"Boy, you get yourself out here now, or I'll give you all of Cooper's chores," the large man bellowed.

The boy sauntered out toward the truck, muttering under his breath, while the man went into the house. The boy's jeans hung low and barely met his wrinkled, white T-shirt. He might have been slightly taller than Cooper. Straggly wet hair hung below his ears.

I tried to slow my breathing; I needed to think. My mind raced and I couldn't focus on anything, so I watched and waited. The boy lifted one cage from the back and then leaned against the truck and lit a cigarette. His back was to me so I decided that this was my chance. I slowly rolled myself out but hit one of the cage's legs with my foot and it made a loud clang. I froze, glad I was in the shadow of a large tree.

Just as I was sure he'd spotted me, I heard a hawk squawking as it swooped low to the truck. The boy grabbed a rake from the back of the truck and waved it crazily at the sleek brown hawk, yelling cuss words. I knew this was my chance. I darted along the other side of the house, scraping my arms on the evergreen and rhododendron bushes, then broke into a run and didn't stop until I ran through my own back door.

I crumpled to the floor; dirt and stink covered me from head to foot. My breath was hard and sharp, and it felt like a huge knife piercing my chest. Lilly nosed around hesitantly, but she must have finally decided it was me because she circled and lay right beside me. My hand went to her back, and I petted her over and over again until my breathing slowed. *I was safe.*

I looked at my scratched arms and dirt-covered clothing and ran upstairs to the bathroom. I ripped off my clothes and turned on the hot water. I couldn't get the stench out of my nose. I couldn't get the hideous pictures out of my mind. I stood with my head under the shower and hoped the water would wash away the smell and pain.

When my sobs subsided, I wrapped myself in a fluffy yellow towel, reached under my bed, and pulled out my mother's tin box. My eyes were still blurred with tears. I'd never felt ready to see what else was in the box, but right now all I could think about is what my mother would do. Lilly came and sat right in front of me, so I patted the carpet next to me so she'd move closer. This time the clippings were held by a new rubber band since the old crusty one had busted. After taking the roll off the top, I removed each item one at a time and laid them in front of me.

One light blue collar with tags dangling, and three small tablets of paper with notes scribbled on most of the pages. A bright green button that said, "Get involved, save a life." Several photos of dogs with labels on the back, and a rose quartz crystal—I know because Henry has a ring with the same stone. I used to hold it up, and when the light shone through I could see a star.

When I reached the bottom, I found a small chain and pulled it up. The pendant on the end was oval made of clear glass with one white swirl. Lilly stood watching the necklace swing back and forth. I caught it with my other hand and looked at it closely before laying it carefully beside the roll of clippings. Lilly nosed it a few times then returned to her place next to me. Another photograph was at the bottom. A baby that I'm sure was me, and Mom. An older woman stood on the front step of a small brick home, her arm around my mother's shoulders.

I scanned the items, hoping to see something that would tell me what to do. I picked up the button and read it aloud: "Get involved, save a life."

If I get involved, I could ruin Cooper's life. He might even get in trouble. I was so afraid that the new friendship we had would be ruined. He'd not only be mad that I had snooped around his house, but he could lose his home altogether. What about the dogs? Some of them are so sick it could be too late already.

I slowly returned each item, saving the pendant for last. I held it up, and the light filtered through so it looked like smoke trapped in glass. I unclasped the ends and put it around my neck, and the cool stone rested against my chest. I'm not sure what I expected; nothing happened. No Harry Potter magic here.

I'm still confused. Getting involved isn't a question, but does that mean I have to choose which life I save?

Chapter 22

I sat down at the table. Henry must have noticed my red eyes and nose because he quietly pulled up a chair and sat across from me. Then his eyes fell to the pendant, his face tensed, and his jaw shifted back and forth.

"Madison, what's wrong?"

When I looked into his eyes, I suddenly felt very small. *He's right; I am still a little kid. I shouldn't have kept any of this from him in the first place.*

"I don't know where to start."

"Just take a breath. Whatever it is, we'll handle it together, OK?" He reached for my hand and held it in his.

"There's a puppy mill, and it's right down the street. Isn't it weird that nobody knows? I don't know what to do." I told him about what I'd seen and he quietly listened, and when I told him about being sick he squeezed my hand harder. "How can we help the dogs without ruining Cooper's life? This is such a mess. I wish I hadn't discovered it."

"Hold on, Madison, one thing at a time. Why don't you start at the beginning?"

I knew he was right. Now wouldn't be a good time to get selective about what information I was going to give him, and I felt comfortable telling him because all the tension in his face had softened.

"Dad, remember when I went to Cooper's last Saturday?" He nodded. "Well, I didn't. I mean, we didn't." *This is it, just spill it.* "We went to Netta's." I looked at him, waiting for a response. He didn't say anything; he just sat there like what I'd said had frozen time. "We rode the bus out on Highway 17 and spent the day helping in the kennels."

"Just once?" he asked, almost like he already knew there was more.

"No, we went another time—a Friday. The one when you went out of town for the day." Again, I waited for him to jump in—he didn't. "We skipped school that day and went to Netta's." *There, it's out. No more secrets.*

"Madison, you have to know this disappoints me, but we'll deal with that later. What does Cooper have to do with the puppy mill?"

"It's his uncle. If they found out that anyone knows they could move again—and take Cooper." My eyes were tearing up again. "Cooper swore he was tired of moving. I didn't understand, but I do now. He said if it happened again, he would get on a bus and disappear." *It would be my fault. This would most certainly be an epic fail on so many levels.*

I wondered if Cooper could be in danger. I was so worried about losing him as a friend that I hadn't even considered that this could be dangerous for him.

Chapter 23

THE NEXT TIME I SAW COOPER IN THE HALL, I TOLD HIM WE NEEDED TO talk and to meet me after school. He shrugged his shoulders and asked why. *What could I say?* We had to talk, even if he didn't want to.

"It's important, Cooper." That's all I said. My stomach tightened as I watched him take in a big breath and let it out quickly, like a deflating balloon. I couldn't tell if he was despondent or relieved. He turned and walked away, his shoulders slumped and his head down.

All I could think about all day was how I was going to tell him that I had been to his place last weekend. I would explain that I had snooped around his yard when I'd thought no one was home and most of all, what I'd seen. All through science I watched him. He avoided me at lunch, and the one time our eyes met, he looked away just like on the first day of school. When school ended I still wasn't very confident about the plan I had for how to tell him. I guess I'd have to spit it all out and pick up the pieces later.

After school we walked to the side of the school where no one would overhear us. "First, I know that I shouldn't have done it, so I'm sorry, but after what you said—and Donald—I just couldn't help myself and when I thought that no one—" The words tumbled out too fast, like little pebbles of information dropping off my tongue and exploding.

"What did you do?" He looked scared. I'd thought that he'd be mad. Instead of the angry eyes I'd expected, they were glassy and dilated.

By now I could tell that he wouldn't be mad, since he was twitching like a trapped rabbit ready to be eaten by a wolf.

"It's OK. I'm not doing anything…yet…I mean, if that's what you're worried about," I said hoping to reassure him. "I went to your house, kind of looking for you, but no one was home and I heard the dogs. I had to check it out; I couldn't help it." He took another deep breath and started walking. I followed.

"I saw the dogs, Cooper. Lots of dogs, and none of them looked very good. It's so sad. Is this what you couldn't explain the other day?" He nodded so I went on. "You know we have to do something. We have to help those dogs, right?"

He stopped and turned to face me, but his eyes avoided mine. "It's always just a matter of time. It always happens."

"What? What happens?"

"I just hoped I could get a year in before we had to move again," he said. If there had been a rock or something to kick, I know he would have kicked it. He wouldn't even look at me.

"I can't," he shook his head.

I felt so bad, but I didn't think we had a choice. I put my hand on his shoulder. "We have to do something—"

"No, no, I meant just me. I can't do it anymore...the moving, the smell, my uncle and my cousin, and especially the dogs. I need to find somewhere to go. I need time." His eyes had taken on a clear look of determination. I hadn't seen it before. With each word he had grown stronger.

"OK, well, how much time do you need? Some of those dogs are barely alive as it is. They're really sick," I said.

"I know. You don't have to tell me."

"I'm not sure what's going to happen. I had to tell my dad." We came to the place where I turned off to go home. "I did ask him to wait until I could warn you."

"Not like I have much of a choice."

"No, you don't—not when all those dogs' lives are at stake," I said. "And besides, Netta will know what to do."

***

On Wednesday we had to get our posts ready and scheduled for the following week. I was prepared to do it alone, but Cooper surprised me when he walked in after school. I'd been scrolling through the comments. Most of them said things like "nice blog," or "interesting," or asked questions like, "can anyone get a foster dog?"There were twenty-two comments, the most we'd ever had. I scrolled through another two or three when one jumped right out at me.

"Cooper, look at this." I pointed to the screen that said, "You're not fooling anyone. I know the truth." It had been left anonymously. "What do you think it means?"

"Sounds to me like we better hurry and wrap this up," he said, rubbing his chin.

I turned to look at him. "Do you think it could be Donald?"

"Maybe, but I'd be surprised."

"Why?" I studied his face but didn't see any answers.

"I just would, especially after last Saturday."

"Yeah, I guess so." I knew that neither of them had been completely honest about what happened that day at the shelter. Ever since "the kennel incident," Donald had steered clear of Cooper.

Chapter 24

The next day Dad drove Cooper and me to Netta's. We rode in silence and stared out the windows. The atmosphere in the car was tense and uncomfortable, like when you know there's something you should be talking about, but you don't talk because it's too much.

When we arrived, Dad said he'd let us explain everything to Netta, so I decided we'd start with the puppies on her doorstep.

"First, Cooper needs to tell you about some of the abandoned puppies you've been finding around your place." I nodded at Cooper.

"*Umm*...well, I put them there. I mean...I rescued them and then made sure you got them, so they'd be safe." He glanced at me and I smiled to assure him he was doing fine. Dad put his hand on my shoulder.

"Where did you rescue them from?" Netta said in a calm tone and offered a chair to Cooper.

"I...I...took them. They weren't being taken care of," he said and slumped into the chair.

"It's OK, Cooper. You're among friends here. Where did the puppies come from?" I could see Cooper opening his mouth but this time no sound came out.

"That's the tough part," I said. "That's why we're here. His uncle runs the puppy mill." I couldn't help it; I just wanted it out. I figured once it was in the open, it wouldn't be the ugly, dark secret that Cooper was choking on.

"Madison, that's a very serious accusation. Cooper, what does she mean?" Netta's eyebrows pinched together.

"She means my uncle's running the puppy mill." His stiff posture and expressionless face made me think of a robot.

"We don't know what to do. Cooper will get into trouble if they knew we were talking." Even now with everything in the light, the hugeness of the problem loomed over us.

"Worse, when they find out that we're discovered, they'll pack up and move," he said. "I'll have to start a new school. At least here I could sneak puppies to Netta. We've moved three times already and I don't—"

"Whoa, OK…OK…Cooper, have you always lived with your uncle?" She took another chair across the table from him. The sun had dropped below the large branches, and golden light reflected off the tears dripping down Cooper's cheeks. He'd softened, surrendered.

"Well, my mom thought it'd be good to stay with my uncle." His voice was choppy and his head was bowed. I looked over at Dad and when his eyes met mine, I knew he was thinking of Mom, just like me.

Henry took another chair and asked, "Do you think you could contact your mom?"

"I've tried." His head shook back and forth until he leaned his elbows on the table and dropped his face into his hands.

Netta stood up. "Anyone hungry? I have some cookies here that aren't too bad if you eat around the burnt parts. I'm not much of a cook, but for some reason the other night I wanted to make cookies. Big mistake. Once I start baking them, I lose interest and start doing something else and I inevitably burn them." It was time for a break, to sit back and look at everything now that it was out in the open. It was a lot to take in.

"I'm starving!" I piped up. I really was. Last night I just hadn't had an appetite at all. Cooper nodded when Netta looked at him, so she gave us both a plate and a glass of milk. Then she flashed a look at Henry.

"Look, I have a few ideas, but right now there's a bunch of hungry dogs that need to be fed. Are you guys up to helping me out?"

"For sure," I said. We stuffed the last of our cookies in our mouths and took our last swigs of milk.

Cooper and I silently fed the dogs. There wasn't anything left to say, at least not until there was some sort of solution. For a moment we stayed silent, holding the reality at bay, even if it was for only a few minutes.

When we'd finished feeding the dogs, Netta waved us to come back into the kitchen. We slipped off our shoes and joined Henry at the table. His notebook was open with all kinds of notes.

"So, what's next?" The short break we'd had in the shelter only punctuated the need for a solution.

"Well, I talked to the ASPCA who put us in contact with a local group. Unfortunately, they can't just go in or prosecute without tangible evidence—"

"I saw it, Dad. Doesn't that count for something? And what's the ASP—whatever?"

"Of course it does, but to make an arrest the department has to get a warrant to search the property." Henry cleared his throat.

"The ASPCA is the American Society for the Protection of Animals," Netta piped in.

"Basically, they need to get a sick animal examined by a vet. There has to be proof that the dog's condition is due to mistreatment. That would give them what they call probable cause, and a judge would grant them a warrant to search the property and seize the dogs," Henry continued. Netta looked at my dad who was biting his bottom lip—something Henry does when he has to talk about something he'd rather not.

"I can do that." Cooper sat up straight. "You only need one?"

"Yes. They said we just need physical evidence of the abuse." Henry put his hand to his mouth, a worried look in his eyes.

"How soon do you need it?" Cooper was standing now, like he was only waiting for the order to march.

"Cooper, you don't have to do this. There are ASPCA investigators who can pose as buyers—"

"It'll take too long to set that up." Cooper was right and Henry knew it. "I got Lilly, didn't I?"

"That was different; she was still a puppy then. We'll need one that is in really bad condition; it won't be easy to sneak that one out."

"I can help him," I said as I stood up.

"No, it's too risky, Madison. I have to do this alone." Cooper's voice sounded different, like taking action lifted the fog of hopelessness he'd had. I knew he was right, and I knew he'd be successful.

"OK, then. Let us know the day you plan to do it, and we can meet you with my truck down the block," Netta said.

I peeked over at Henry, who was staring intently into Cooper's eyes. When he placed his hands on Cooper's shoulders he said, "You don't have to do this. If you change your mind, or get caught—"

"I won't."

Chapter 25

The phone call came during the night. When my cell phone rang, I grabbed it on the first ring. It was Cooper; he was breathing heavily.

"Everyone's asleep. I tried Netta's but she doesn't answer. This is my chance. I snuck the dog out and hid her in my room so I didn't have to disturb the other dogs. I'm afraid she's too sick to wait until morning. Can your dad come?" It was hard to hear his whisper between breaths.

"Sure, I'll wake him. We'll get there as soon as we can. We'll park down the road around the corner on Elm, OK?" I realized I was whispering for no reason. I hung up and went to wake Henry.

"Dad, Dad, wake up." I shook his shoulder. When his eyes didn't open, I shook harder. "Dad—Henry—we have to go get Cooper."

"What, now? In the middle of the night?" he asked, sitting up on the side of the bed. I'd already gathered a T-shirt, jeans, and his shoes.

"He didn't have a choice, but we have to leave now." I helped him with his shirt and then headed for the stairs. "Come on, Dad."

"I'm coming, I'm coming." We tumbled out of the house and into the car.

"I told him to meet us at Stuart and Elm, just around the corner. He's afraid the dog won't make it through the night." I was panting and finding it hard to catch my breath.

We rounded the corner and headed toward Elm. It was dark, but the moon threw just enough of a glow that we could turn off our lights while we waited. We'd barely parked when we saw Cooper stepping out from behind some bushes.

"How long have you been sitting there?" Henry asked.

"Not long. We better hurry, though. She's hardly breathing." I recognized the dog in Cooper's arms. She was the one that had her nose and mouth wrapped shut. Now her jaw just hung like it was broken.

"Do you think we can make it?" I asked. Dad had already dialed Netta and was waiting for her to answer.

"Netta, sorry to call so late, but it's an emergency. Cooper has rescued one of the dogs, but she's in such bad shape she may not make it to morning...uh-huh...OK...see you soon." He put his phone down and pointed to the backseat. "You need to wrap her in that blanket. Do you know if she's been able to eat or drink?"

Cooper shook his head and wrapped her in the green army blanket. I'd forgotten about it; it's been years since we had a reason to use the blanket. There are pictures of baby-me and Mom sitting on it at the beach. I remembered that it felt scratchy on my bare legs.

"I doubt it. Her bowl was empty," said Cooper. I stroked her ears and the top of her head. She seemed to relax.

"Netta says if we can get her through the night, the vet will be there first thing in the morning." Dad accelerated onto Highway 17.

As I stroked the dog, I started to pick up images—flashes, really, like the camera shutter on Henry's old Minolta. They were black and white. One of the flashes gave me a huge jabbing pain in the back of my throat, and I started to cough.

"You all right?" Cooper asked.

"I think so…did something happen to her throat?" I rubbed my neck just under my chin.

"Yeah. How did you know?"

"I feel it." I'm sure my pain wasn't as bad, but it felt like something extremely hot had gone down my throat.

"My cousin did it. He shoved a broom handle into her mouth just because she was barking. I tried nursing her back to health, but I could only do so much."

As the pain dulled in my throat, the sadness inside began to spread out from my chest like cold soda. *How could anyone do something so mean?*

Chapter 26

Dad was on the phone with Netta the next two nights. The vet had determined that the dog's condition was due to neglect and abuse, but unfortunately was unable to save it. Dad said they were working with local authorities. Cooper, on the other hand, had dropped out of sight. He hadn't been at school at all, and I was worried that we were too late and his uncle had already moved the dogs. Which meant more dogs could die.

On Friday, Cooper slunk in just before the bell and slid into his seat. He looked worse than usual. His clothes had that wrinkled, dirty look they'd had the first couple of days of school. He looked tired, and his eyes were dull. I was glad to see him because now I could tell him what Henry had said.

Last night I'd asked Henry what would happen to Cooper I'd hoped that the plan included the answer to the dog's problem and to Cooper's.

"Well, there are a few options, but they're entirely up to Cooper. Your job is to bring him home after school so we can set the plan in motion."

A small flutter pulsed through me. We had a plan—and not just for the dogs. I knew that after this, things between Dad and me would be different. Everything was going to be different.

When the bell rang everyone poured into the hall. I followed Cooper and tugged on his shirt. "Hey, where've you been? We have a lot to do on our blog." He stopped and turned to look at me, and his red eyes made mine water. I knew he had more important things on his mind than a dumb old class blog.

"Are you OK?"

"Not really...tried to get my mom; the number said it was disconnected."

"I'm sorry, Cooper. We need to talk to my dad. He and Netta have been on the phone every night, and I think there's a plan. They're waiting for me—I mean, us," I said and he looked up. "They wanted to give you time to reach your mother."

"Thanks...don't matter." He took a deep breath and let it out slowly. I could tell he believed he was out of options, and no matter how much he'd wanted to find his mother, it just wasn't going to happen.

"Of course it matters; you can't go back. It isn't your fault, and besides I...I don't want you to leave." I looked at his face and realized in that moment that he was my friend and I couldn't let anything happen to him. "You have to come with me."

Chapter 27

Netta and Dad were sitting at the table when we walked through the door. "Hi, Madison, Cooper. Today is the day," Netta said, standing. Dad stood, too, and we all went into the living room.

"The authorities have the warrant but have given us some extra time when we explained your situation. They didn't want to move in until you had time to settle your position. The last thing anyone wants is to endanger a child's welfare in the process of protecting the animals," Dad said and cleared his throat. "Now, have you been able to find your mother?"

"No. I only had a phone number. My uncle has no idea where she is." Cooper looked from me to Dad and back to me again. He picked at the hem of his shirt and stared at the floor. I thought he must feel very alone. His life was going to change. Even though it might seem better to us, he doesn't know for sure. He must feel like he's jumping off a cliff into an unknown abyss.

"The Department of Social Services—the government agency for children's welfare—will step in as soon as your uncle is arrested. Our idea—well, of course, everything is totally up to you—but Netta really needs help at the shelter." Dad looked over to Netta.

"That's right, and I have extra room. It will be harder for you to get to school, but you're already familiar with the bus system—both of you." She winked at me and then looked anxiously at Cooper. "Now, we'll keep trying to find your mother, but in the meantime you can stay with me. What do you think?" She bit her bottom lip, waiting for his answer.

"That's an awful lot to ask of someone, especially you. You have all those dogs to take—"

"No, no, not at all. I need help; and besides, it can get lonely out there with just me and the dogs." She looked at Cooper. "Most important, it will give you a safe place to be until the dust settles."

I thought this sounded like a great idea, but Cooper didn't look so confident. I decided it would be worse not knowing where the heck your mother is. At least I've always known where my mother was—even if I couldn't see her. I realized that Cooper's situation was just as dire as the dogs'. He needed to be rescued, too.

"What happens when I don't find her?" His head bowed limply. He looked tired and I knew he hadn't slept in a while.

"Well," Netta said and walked over to Lilly. "That, Cooper, is something we aren't going to worry about right now.

The important thing is that you're safe." She made a quick check of Lilly's ears and each paw. "Madison's dad and I will take care of contacting the authorities. And Cooper—" She placed her hands on his shoulders and looked into his eyes. "Everything's going to be fine." Somehow hearing Netta say it made it seem like maybe, just maybe, things would work out.

Cooper didn't say anything, but that was fine because we all knew he needed time to think. Then he stood up. "Can I take Lilly for a walk?"

"Sure." When I stood up to join him, he gave me a look that said he wanted to be alone. I watched out the window as he and Lilly walked across the lawn to the sidewalk. As usual, Lilly had to stop and mark the telephone pole at the corner of our yard. Cooper waited patiently before heading down the sidewalk. His shoulders were hunched and he bowed his head, reminding me of how he looked on the first day of school. Even though I knew this was what we had to do, it didn't ease the guilt that weighed on me. I guess the reality is that just because you're making the right decision, doesn't make it any easier.

***

Dad said it all happened very quickly. The police went in and immediately arrested Cooper's uncle. Within two days, the dogs had all been transferred to Netta's. She had called several other shelters, and they said they had room for more and would pick up the dogs during the next week.

Over the next weekend, Cooper and I created a whole blog post using news articles and information from our research to let people know what had happened. On Monday the local newspaper, *The Hawthorne Herald*, came to the school to take our pictures. Mr. Pinehurst, the principal, directed them personally to our classroom. This was a big deal!

"Is it true you discovered this operation all on your own?" the reporter asked, scratching something down on his pad of paper.

"Well, kinda—I mean it was both of us, Cooper and I, that reported it." I looked over to Cooper hoping he would say something, but his eyes were glued to the floor and his mouth was frozen in a fake smile. I knew the smile wasn't real because I've seen him smile, and he usually shows his teeth.

For the rest of the day when we walked down the hall kids would look at us and sometimes asked us how we did it. It made me uncomfortable to have the attention. Cooper usually let me do the talking and stood nervously next to me. *So much for invisibility.* Paige and even her new friends stopped us to ask what they could do to help.

Netta helped us get pictures of several of the dogs to post on our blog so we could find homes for them. We received many comments from readers who were interested in helping, so we posted the address and phone number of the Second Chance Shelter. In one week we had over a thousand views and over fifty comments, many offering to help either by taking a dog or sending money to help Netta with the shelter. There were so many awesome people out there willing to help.

We received another anonymous comment that said, "Don't forget that there are still others out there who need help." Cooper and I wondered what it was supposed to mean. Help with what? Who needs help?

Chapter 28

Dad and I have been out to the shelter every weekend. Today when we arrived, the in-the-kennels sign was on the door. We walked in and heard Netta.

"It's all about energy; dogs pick up on our energy. Have you ever seen a dog jumping around like crazy while on a leash with its owner? Well, it isn't the dog that has issues; it's the person." She stood just outside the door of the kennel, quietly waiting for the dog to come to her. Once the dog approached her, she gently opened the gate and waited again until the dog was relaxed. Then she attached the leash and handed it to Cooper.

As Cooper took the leash the dog was calm; I knew it because I could feel it. That meant Cooper was calm—something that I hadn't seen for a long time.

As we drove home and passed Paige's house, I heard laughter and screaming coming from her backyard. I knew that she and all her new friends were out jumping on her trampoline. The funny thing was, it didn't really bother me.

We're just interested in different things and that's OK. Besides, I have a great new friend. *Even if he is a boy.*

Things that have changed:

Cooper is safe at Netta's.

I'm finally having fun training Lilly.

Dad and I are talking more about Mom.

After Lilly's walk, I went upstairs. The walls still looked babyish, but it didn't matter anymore. Now I knew that my mom had decorated the room, and I liked seeing her in the pink flowers. *I still think the paintball idea would be cool, but I can wait until the time is right.*

Later that night Dad and I sat in the family room. Lilly sat next to me licking her paws, one and then the other. In that moment, I realized that she was mine and I was hers, and it was time to adopt her and make her a permanent part of our family.

The newspaper was spread out on the carpet, and I was cutting out the picture of Cooper and me. The caption read, "Local Heroes Rescue over 100 Puppies."

"Your mother would be so proud of you," Dad said and joined me on the floor. I opened Mom's tin box and was about to place the new article on top when he pulled out the roll of Mom's older clips. He stared at it, tears running down his face.

"Your mother had a gift, Madison."

"I know, Dad. I have it, too."

Resources

These are just a few of the places you can go to get involved in the cause of animals. You can find further resources on Madison's Website at www.madisonmorgan11.com.

The American Society For The Prevention of Cruelty to Animals

http://www.aspca.org/

Founded in 1866, the ASPCA was the first humane organization in the Western Hemisphere. Our mission, as stated by founder Henry Bergh, is "to provide effective means for the prevention of cruelty to animals throughout the United States." The ASPCA works to rescue animals from abuse, pass humane laws and share resources with shelters nationwide.

The Humane Society of The United States

http://www.humanesociety.org/

The Humane Society of the United States is the nation's largest and most effective animal protection organization, backed by 11 million Americans. We help animals by advocating for better laws to protect animals; conducting campaigns to reform industries; providing animal rescue and emergency response; investigating cases of animal cruelty; and caring for animals through our sanctuaries and wildlife rehabilitation centers, emergency shelters and clinics.

International Fund For Animal Welfare

http://www.ifaw.org/us/

Founded in 1969, the International Fund for Animal Welfare saves individual animals, animal populations and habitats all over the world. With projects in more than 40 countries, IFAW provides hands-on assistance to animals in need, whether it's dogs and cats, wildlife and livestock, or rescuing animals in the wake of disasters. We also advocate saving populations from cruelty and depletion, such as our campaign to end commercial whaling and seal hunts.

Made in the USA
Charleston, SC
24 July 2012